D1572441

A WHIRLWIND YEAR OF
EXCITEMENT AND YOUNG LOVE...

Here is an utterly charming story of the mischief and romance of junior year in Paris.

Written with the same warm sensitivity that Norma Klein has brought to her other bestselling Fawcett novels *It's OK If You Don't Love Me* and *Love Is One of the Choices*, FRENCH POSTCARDS is an entrancing look at the most romantic city in the world through the eyes of young lovers who want to experience it all.

FRENCH POSTCARDS

A Novel By

Norma Klein

Based on the motion picture by

Willard Huyck
and Gloria Katz

Fawcett Gold Medal • New York

FRENCH POSTCARDS

© 1979 Paramount Pictures Corporation

Published by Fawcett Gold Medal Books, a unit of CBS Publications, the Consumer Publishing Division of CBS Inc.

ISBN: 0-449-14297-3

Printed in the United States of America

10 9 8 7 6 5 4 3 2 1

For Lora and Allan

1

"God, I wish she'd stop talking for one second," Melanie said. "I can't even concentrate on Paris with her babbling away like that."

"It's good for our French," Laura whispered back.

"Yeah, I guess."

Laura looked toward the front of the bus, where Madame Tessier, the head of the Institute for French Studies, was standing, holding a microphone. She spoke rapidly and crisply, flashing her dark eyes at the busload of American students who had just arrived the day before for their junior year abroad. Laura watched her in fascination. Typically French. If you were American and in your mid-thirties, she thought, you were frazzled from two kids and diapers and trying to hold down a job at the same time, like her older sister, Meg.

Madame Tessier looked like she was *never* frazzled. She looked as though any crisis would find her cool, impeccably groomed, her eye makeup perfectly in place. Maybe I'll get to be like that after I'm here a few months, she thought wistfully.

"She's beautiful, isn't she?" she said to Melanie.

"Who?"

"Her—Madame Tessier."

Melanie gave Madame Tessier a long, appraising glance. "If you like that type, I guess," she said, evidently unimpressed.

Melanie was a cool customer herself, Laura had discovered. They were going to be roommates and had begun talking together on the plane the day before. Melanie was pretty—fluffy dark hair, a slightly sardonic expression in her brown eyes. On the plane she had made disparaging comments about all the boys. "God, where did they find them? You'd think they would have come up with at least *one* sexy one! *Look* at them!" Laura had confided that she didn't mind that much because she was going steady with someone at home. "Going *steady?*" Melanie had exclaimed. "I didn't know people did that anymore." "Well, I mean, we just go out just with each other," Laura said. Melanie had seemed vaguely impressed. "True love, huh?" she said. Laura had blushed. "We really like each other," she admitted. "Is he a good lover?" Melanie had wanted to know right away. Laura had swallowed nervously, unused to this degree of candor on the basis of a two-hour friendship. "I guess I don't know," she admitted. "How come? Aren't you even sleeping together?" "Yeah, we are," Laura said, "but I never did it with anyone else, so I don't have any point of comparison." "Oh, right, I get it."

Melanie had gone on to tell Laura all about her erstwhile boyfriend, Frank, whom her parents thought was a real hippie just because, Melanie said, "his hair is down to his shoulders. They are *so* prejudiced, you wouldn't believe it! And so uptight about sex! When they found out we were doing it, they practically went after him with a shotgun! When I told them we were only doing it because I wanted to as much as him, Mom almost had a *cow!* She gave me this whole spiel about birth control and did I realize it was a woman's responsibility to set the limits. All kinds of garbage like that. She's as sexist as Daddy, worse, I sometimes think."

While she had talked, Laura had started thinking about David, even though she had promised herself that she wouldn't do that. She knew she might try to use him as an excuse for not getting involved in anything in Paris. Her father, whom she was close to, had spoken to her about it before she left. "Darling, you're only nineteen," he said, "and David is a fine person, but . . . well, why not take this chance to see how you feel about other boys? If you really love him and still want to marry him after a year apart, that will prove it's more than just puppy love."

Puppy love! She could have *killed* her father for saying that. What she and David had was certainly not puppy love! So what if they were both nineteen? It wasn't just physical attraction, like Melanie

9

with Frank. It was real *love*. They stayed up late at night and read Keats together. She knitted him socks. He bought her lemon cologne and lovingly dabbed it behind her ears. They were tender and caring with each other. Even in making love. It wasn't just jumping into bed with someone. Neither of them was like that. It was serious. Sure, she could see that most people needed time to grow up and find out who they were, as her father said. But she and David were mature for their ages. They might be nineteen in *fact,* but in outlook they were as good as twenty-five or thirty. We'll show them, Laura thought. They were going to write every single day!

David's parents were exactly the same! They wanted him to go out with other girls, since Cornell was co-ed. His brother, who was a senior, had actually tried to fix him up on a double date practically before she had left! "He is gross," David had said. "He just doesn't know. He thinks we're just sleeping together, like him and Judy. He doesn't know this is the real thing."

They were both sorry that no one seemed to understand. Clearly, no one they knew had ever been through anything like this, so of *course* they were jealous, of *course* they didn't understand. "We'll show them," David had said. "I'm not going to even go out with anyone the whole time you're gone." "Well, you could just go *out* with people," Laura suggested, pleased at what he'd said. "Just, like, to the movies or something." "No," he insisted. "What's the point? I can go to the movies alone or with Jon. Face it, after you, they all seem like total nonentities. I'd be bored." Laura had beamed.

The bus was passing down the Champs-Élysées. The magnificent, wide street excited Laura, she felt they were at the heart of Paris, as she had imagined it would be. At the end of the street she could see the Arc de Triomphe.

"That's where the eternal flame is lit," she said breathlessly to Melanie.

"Huh?"

"On the Tomb of the Unknown Soldier," Laura said. "He's buried under the Arc de Triomphe. God, I feel so excited, finally seeing all these things! Don't you?"

"Sure, kind of," Melanie agreed.

How could she be so casual? Everything Laura saw—the glimpse of the flowers in the Tuileries gardens—seemed like some magical color postcard come to life. It had all been here, waiting for her. It was just as beautiful as she had imagined, more so because it was real.

"You have come from America to study in France," Madame Tessier was saying. "And no matter what you do later in life, you will remember the year you spent here and it will change you." The bus began moving faster. The driver honked his horn. Madame Tessier seemed on the verge of losing some of her composure. But then went on smoothly, "You will start to think in French because we are going to aim at nothing less than the total experience of becoming French. From this moment you must wipe everything American from your mind as you immerse yourself in the sophistication, the depth, the subtle elegance of French culture."

"Hey, *there's* someone I'd like to immerse myself in," Melanie whispered. She had the window seat. She nudged Laura and pointed to a Frenchman who was walking along the sidewalk, whistling jauntily. "Gee, he's cute." As she spoke, the man looked up and saw the two of them staring. He smiled and waved. Melanie waved back. "Hey, how terrific, he noticed us! Oh, no, I'll never see him again!"

"There'll be others," Laura said, consolingly.

"That cute?" Melanie said woefully as the bus made a turn and the Frenchman vanished from sight.

"Sure," Laura said. "I didn't think he was *that* cute. . . . David's much better looking," she added.

"Do you have a picture of him?" Melanie asked.

Laura nodded. She took from her wallet the one she'd taken of him when they went on a picnic that spring. It showed him sitting under a tree, gazing soulfully at the sky. "Usually he wears glasses," she admitted, "but he looks nice without them too."

Melanie inspected the photo carefully. "Cute," she said offhandedly. "I guess you like the sensitive type, huh?"

Laura hadn't thought of it that way. "I guess," she said.

"I like boys—men—with more . . . pizzazz," she said. "*You* know, with kind of a gleam in their eye, like they're ready for fun. Frank was like that. You knew he'd do anything on a dare."

"David is more . . . introspective," Laura said.

"Yeah, well, you seem that way too, so I guess you're well suited . . . You're really serious, huh?"

Laura nodded. "We want to get married as soon as we graduate. I'm going to get a doctorate in medieval studies and he's going to go to architecture school."

Melanie whistled. "Heavy! Two intellectuals! Well, I guess it's good you, you know, have the same goals and all that."

"We've even decided the names of our children," Laura confessed. "Of course we won't have them for ten years, but we decided on Angela for the girl and Daniel for the boy."

"Boy, you are really different from me," Melanie exclaimed. "Planning that far ahead! I don't even know what's going to happen the next week!"

"Oh, look!" Laura exclaimed. "Look at the fountains!"

They were at the Place de la Concorde. "They're pretty," Melanie agreed.

"I can't wait to see them at night!" Laura said. "They're supposed to be really beautiful. They light them up."

"How do you know all this stuff?" Melanie said.

"Oh, I read all about it," Laura said. "I love the way everything sounds in French. *'Fontaine lumineuse de la Concorde.'* Don't you love the way that sounds? It's so much prettier than just 'lighted fountain.' "

13

She gazed with fascination at the Egyptian obelisk of Luxor, rising in the center of the fountains. To one side was the Seine, flowing along calmly, as though it didn't even realize it was anything special. It just thought it was another river. I want to have a picnic there, Laura thought, and I'll pretend David is with me. Paris is for lovers—that's what they said. The thought gave her a pang.

Suddenly a loud blaring of rock music came soaring from the front of the bus. The driver had turned on the radio. Madame Tessier sat down, defeated.

"You know what this reminds me of?" Laura said.

"What? Who?"

"No, I mean this whole thing, our coming to Paris. It reminds me of my mother's favorite movie, *Sabrina*. Did you ever see that?"

Melanie shook her head.

"It's with Audrey Hepburn. She was my mother's favorite actress, and she goes to Paris for a year to study cooking, and when she is about to come back she writes this letter to her father saying how being in Paris has taught her all about life and how to live. And she becomes this really glamorous, sophisticated-looking woman, and this rich guy she was in love with sees her at the train station and doesn't even *recognize* her because she's so glamorous! And he falls madly in love with her even though she's poor."

Melanie sighed. "Maybe that'll happen to us. Do you think it will? I mean, becoming sophisticated

14

and chic and all? They say French women always look great even when they're just slopping around. They know what to buy even when they have no money . . . Like, look at her!" She pointed out the window at a young woman who was walking briskly in a flowered print dress, her hair swept up jauntily, high-heeled sandals on her feet.

"She looks very sure of herself," Laura said.

"Yeah . . . They *all* look like that. Well, I guess they *are* sure of themselves. I think it's because they have all these wiles to use on men that they learn when they're practically in the cradle."

"I don't like that, though," Laura said. "The idea of using wiles. I believe in being straightforward."

"Do you?" Melanie said in surprise. "I wouldn't mind having a *few* wiles. . . . Maybe I'll learn some while I'm here, you know, like putting perfume on the soles of my feet or something."

"The soles of your feet?" Laura said. "Why there?"

"Oh, I don't know. No special reason . . . So someone can kiss my toes."

Laura had never thought of that. She didn't like her feet. She didn't even like to *think* of someone kissing her toes.

"I once read this article in *Cosmo,*" Melanie said, "about this woman who got an orgasm just from someone kissing her big toe!"

"Really?" Laura said, impressed. "Did he do it in some special way?"

"I guess . . . Or else she just had very sensitive toes . . . Well, they say there are all kinds of, you know, erogenous zones that are different for every-one. Ears or belly buttons or anything!"

"I think my ears are sensitive," Laura mused, remembering how David used to kiss her earlobes.

"I have just *got* to have an affair with a French man," Melanie exclaimed. "I mean, I want someone who really knows the ropes. Frank was okay, but—"

"How about us?" someone said in back of them. Laura and Melanie turned around. It was a shaggy-haired blond boy named Alex whom they had met on the plane. He was sitting next to a sort of funny-looking dark-haired boy whose name Laura didn't know.

"Have you been listening to our whole conversation?" Melanie demanded.

"Well, as much of it as we could hear over Madame Tessier," Alex admitted.

"Boy!" Melanie said. "Some nerve!"

Laura blushed to think they had heard all about David. She glanced away.

"*We're* sexy," Alex said, grinning. "What do you need with a French man?"

"You?" Melanie said scornfully. "Hah!"

"What do you mean—hah?" Alex said. "Look at us. Poised, debonair."

"Sure," Melanie said.

"You just want some guy with a French accent who'll kiss your big toe!" Alex said, smiling. He looked at Laura. He has a nice smile, she thought.

"Look, there are plenty of guys like you back home," Melanie said. "I want something different.

Don't *you*?" she said. "I mean, don't you want to meet some sexy French girl?"

"Sounds okay to me," Joel said. He seemed shyer than Alex.

"How about *her?*" Melanie went on, pointing to the front of the bus.

"Who?"

"What's her name. With the microphone."

"She's beautiful," Alex admitted, "but she probably has around ten lovers already."

"Maybe, maybe not," Melanie said. "Why don't you ask her?"

Alex looked at her, amazed. "I'm supposed to just walk up to her and say, 'Hey, I'm interested in having an affair with you. Do you have a lover? If not, I'm available.' "

"Sure, why not?" Melanie said. "What can you lose?"

Alex looked reflective. "True . . . I guess I don't have the nerve."

"Well, if *you* don't, someone will," Melanie said. She turned around to face front again. "Hey, I think we're finally here. Finally! I'm really getting stiff. Oh look, do you think that's Monsieur Tessier? He's not so sexy. Darn!"

Laura followed her meekly out of the bus. She was overwhelmed at Melanie's *savoir faire* and ease with boys, even ones she didn't know. I'll never be like that, she thought. Well, anyway, David doesn't mind, she consoled herself. He likes me just the way I am.

2

Joel and Alex stood for a moment, bewildered by the noise and confusion in the large room. It was like the entrance hall to a palace—high ceilings, marble floors, windows stretching up almost from the floor. But the elegance of the room was belied by the atmosphere. Small tables had been set up around the room, and at each one a French student sat, giving advice and instructions to the lines of American students streaming in. On each desk were piles of papers and cards.

"It's like freshman orientation," Joel said.

"It's a great room, though, don't you think?" Alex said, gazing up at the baroque-looking ceiling. At home, freshman orientation had been held in the college gym, which hadn't been too heavy on atmosphere.

"She's too much!" Joel said.

"Who?"

"The one with the dark hair . . . She reminds me of my sister."

"The other one was pretty," Alex said.

"Yeah, only she has that boyfriend, David."

"True. . . . Well, maybe she'll forget about him after a while."

"It sounded pretty serious to me," Joel said.

"I wonder if she's right about, you know, Madame Tessier . . . What do you think?"

"She *is* beautiful," Joel said gravely. "I don't know. I wouldn't think she'd bother with someone like us."

"They say women like younger men, though," Alex said. "I read somewhere that in terms of sex the best relationship is between a seventeen-year-old boy and a thirty-five-year-old woman, because they're both at their sexual peak."

Joel gazed over at Madame Tessier, who was standing at a desk, handing out papers. "She looks at *her* sexual peak," he said. "I don't know about me."

"You haven't had a chance to find out yet," Alex said.

"True," Joel said. He looked doleful. "I don't know. I bet it's going to be the same over here as in the States. All the girls will go for some big jock type."

"No," Alex said. "Look at what that blond girl said on the bus . . . She likes sensitive types."

"Yeah, she *says* that," Joel said, "but David is probably six feet tall and really handsome. If all he

-did was read Keats, I bet she wouldn't even look at him."

"You just don't have enough self-confidence when it comes to girls," Alex said.

"True," Joel admitted.

"I mean, look at me. *I'm* not that handsome or anything, but I've done all right. It's mainly a matter of self-confidence."

"Yeah, but that's the trouble," Joel said. "What if you don't have any?"

"Pretend you do," Alex suggested.

Joel sighed. "Well, yeah . . . I could try. I doubt I'd convince anyone, though. I bet any girl would see through me in three seconds flat."

They got on line to receive their papers.

"Student identification, *carte de séjour,* university restaurant tickets, schedule of classes . . ."

Amidst the confusion, Alex found himself looking over at Madame Tessier. She was standing talking to a French girl. She's too pretty, he thought. Christ, she's beautiful. She's not even just pretty. Up until that moment it had seemed to him that his feminine ideal was Jacqueline Bisset as she had looked in *The Deep,* with her smoldering dark eyes, soft hair, and her incredible figure showing through her wet T-shirt. I wonder how *she'd* look in a wet T-shirt, he thought. Then he remembered what the girl on the bus had said. Just go over to her? And say what? Here I am, the love of your life, the guy you've been waiting for?

First of all, she was probably madly in love with her husband. And if she wasn't, she probably had a lover already, at least one, a suave, dapper type who knew how to give her an orgasm by kissing her big toe. What does she need *you* for? Still, it was true, it couldn't hurt to try. Mustering his courage, he went over to where she was standing.

"I—um—can't seem to find my luggage," he said.

"Your luggage?" She looked alarmed. "Is it lost?"

"I don't know . . . No one seems to know where it is."

She sighed. "Oh, goodness . . . Albertine! This student here—what did you say your name was?"

"Alex . . . Alex Jensen."

"He cannot find his luggage!" she said, gesticulating. "What next? Can't they *ever* do this right?" To Alex, she said, "Stay here, please. I am terribly sorry for this inconvenience. I wish I could say it is rare. In fact, it seems to happen all the time."

"Oh, that's okay," Alex said graciously. He was content to stand beside her, glancing at her as often as he could without seeming obvious. She had beautiful shiny black hair. It caught the light. I wonder if she's read any of those studies about seventeen-year-old boys and thirty-five-year-old women, he wondered.

"You are from what university?" she asked.

"Oberlin."

"Ah, yes." But she looked a little confused.

"It's in Ohio," he said. "It's a small school."

"Yes? I have heard of it, of course . . . But perhaps because it is small, there are not so many students coming from there. The educational quality is very high, no doubt?"

"Yes, it's pretty—it's a good school," he stammered.

Suddenly she smiled at him for no reason he could fathom. His heart turned over. "You are looking forward to your year in Paris?" she asked.

"Oh, yes, a lot!" he said eagerly. "My father teaches French, actually. That's one reason he—my parents—wanted me to come."

"Oh? At a university?"

"No, at a—um—high school . . . But he and my mother speak it pretty well . . . I think," he added honestly, since he wasn't sure he'd be able to tell if they were speaking badly.

"And your French? How is it? Fluent?"

Alex flushed. If only he'd studied harder! "Not exactly fluent," he admitted.

"You'll pick it up very quickly, don't worry," she said in a soft, caressing voice. "You'll find yourself a French girl and she will teach you everything."

I want you to teach me everything, Alex thought. He tried desperately to think of something witty or interesting to say. "I guess French girls will be different from American ones," was all he could manage.

"You think so?" She acted as though he had made a profound observation. "Well, in details perhaps, but we are all sisters under the skin, I'm sure."

Emboldened, he went on. "French girls—

women—seem . . . well, more elegant. Like you!" he suddenly blurted out.

She smiled. "How nice! You think I am elegant? I'll have to remember that when I am feeling especially—how do you say—out of it?"

"Well, I mean, compared to the—um—women I know, like my teachers and my mother and girls in my school, you seem . . . different. I guess I can't explain it." He felt desperate. "You have a nice smell."

This time she burst out laughing, but in a nice way. "Well, that is very perceptive. You've noticed I am wearing a new cologne this morning for the first time. You must have a very sensitive nose."

Alex blushed. "I don't know," he admitted.

She patted his arm. "Don't worry. You'll have some little French girl entranced in no time at all. . . . Now, I'm sorry, if you'll excuse me, I have some details to attend to. Wait here and I will check back later about your luggage."

In a daze, Alex watched her walk off. His eyes followed her as she moved gracefully across the room and was then hidden from sight.

"Hey, how's it going?" It was Joel.

"What?"

"Did you find your luggage?"

"Uh . . . I don't know."

"What d'you mean you don't know? Did you find it or not?"

"They're looking," Alex said, still half in a trance.

"What's wrong with you? Are you okay?"

Alex looked at him. "She spoke to me."

"Who? What the hell are you talking about?"

"Madame Tessier . . . She said I had a sensitive nose."

Joel shook his head. "You're crazy . . . How come she said that?"

"We had a real conversation," Alex said. "Her English is really good . . . Oh God, do you think she has a lover?"

"I don't know," Joel said. "I guess so."

"Maybe that's a stereotype," Alex said. "It's just something they say. She might be different."

"What good will that do you?"

"Well, maybe I'll be the first one . . . I mean, maybe she'll—I don't know."

"It's a nice fantasy," Joel said.

"You think that's all it is? A fantasy, huh?"

"Well, yeah . . . But we've only been here one day."

"Her husband looks like a real bastard," Alex said. "I heard him chewing out some kids who didn't have the right papers. Just like our principal in high school, Mr. Jordan . . . Why did she marry him?"

"I don't know," Joel said. "Maybe he's different with her."

"I bet she hates him," Alex went on. "She *has* to! She probably married him when she was really young and didn't know any better. Now she's really fed up, now that she's realized what he's like."

"I guess that's possible," said Joel.

"She has this kind of lonely expression," Alex said. "Sort of . . . wistful."

"Yeah?"

"Yeah . . . Her eyes. She has beautiful eyes." He blinked. "Well, I guess you're right. It's all a fantasy."

"Fantasies aren't bad," Joel said. "I didn't mean to say that."

"They just aren't real," Alex said, sighing. "That's the trouble with them."

"Ah, monsieur, your luggage . . . we have traced it." A young Frenchman smiled at him.

"Great," Alex said. "I've only got the clothes I'm wearing and—"

"I regret, monsieur, but your luggage went on to Russia."

"Russia?" said Joel.

"We will recover it as soon as possible."

Alex grinned. "It's lucky I really like these clothes."

*   *   *

That afternoon all the students met in the institute's salon. Alex watched Monsieur Tessier stride into the room. He stood stiffly behind the lectern, trying to smile. It looked like a smile that had been glued on his face. Madame Tessier stood to one side, watching him thoughtfully.

"*Je sème une graine qui pourra un jour produire une moisson,*" recited Monsieur Tessier. He looked around the room, like a hawk waiting to decide what mouse to pounce on. His eyes rested on Alex. "Would you translate please, monsier?"

Alex stared at him. He hadn't heard a thing. "Um—why me?" he said. He smiled nervously. "*Pourquoi moi?*"

There was quiet laughter around the room.

"Why you?" Monsieur Tessier said. "Do you mean, was it just a random choice or was it the vacuous expression on your face—which makes me suspect that behind it lies an equally vacuous brain!"

"Albert," Madame Tessier murmured disapprovingly.

But he continued in the same vein, pushing through the seated students towards Alex. "Why you?" he said again. "Perhaps years of teaching have given me a sixth sense—I instantly perceive the intellectually underdeveloped! *Comme vous, monsieur. Dites moi la vérité, vous n'êtes pas vraiment un étudiant!*"

"Uh—*non, monsieur,*" Alex stammered. "I mean, *oui, monsieur.*" He looked around desperately for assistance.

Madame Tessier caught her husband by the arm. "Just give them the speech we planned," she said curtly.

"What's the use?" he said, exasperated. "They understand nothing! Look at them! Imbeciles!"

"Albert, please! Do you wish *me* to give the speech?"

"No!" He retreated behind the lectern again. "So you have come from different American universities

27

to study at our institute. I assume my wife, Madame Tessier, has told you that we provide a classical education. Now, I know that in some of your universities there are no grades. Or, if you don't like your grades, you just drop it: poof!" He slammed his hand down. "Well, I am sorry, but that does not happen here!"

"Albert?" Madame Tessier called softly, but he went on imperturbably.

"I even read that in your country the students decide the curriculum! The students say, 'Oh, no, we don't want literature, no philosophy for us this year . . . We think we will study . . . mushrooms!" His voice rose. "Mushrooms! I have news for you! Here, at *my* school, you will not study mushrooms!"

Joel nudged Alex. "He's really crazy."

"Yeah, I feel sorry for her."

During the rest of the lecture Alex stared at Madame Tessier. It seemed to him her face had a sad, critical expression as she watched her husband. Why did she marry someone like that? he wondered.

When the lecture ended, he started out, but she came up to him. "I am so sorry," she said in a soft lilting voice. "You must excuse my husband. His nerves are not always so . . . rested on the first day."

"Oh, that's okay," Alex said. "I guess I wasn't really listening . . . I should have been."

"It's hard in the beginning," she said. "You still

think in English . . . But after a while, you'll see, you'll even *dream* in French!"

He smiled. I'll dream about you! he thought, and then blushed, as though she could hear his thoughts.

"You and your friend are settled in your new home?"

"Uh—yes," Alex said. "It's a nice place."

"Good . . . We try and provide the best accommodations. I'm glad you are comfortable . . . Well!" She smiled up at him. "Let me know if there is anything I can help you with. Remember, we are always here, always at your disposal!"

"Okay, I'll remember," Alex said.

When she walked off, Joel, who had been standing beside him, said, "Hey, maybe she does like you!"

Alex sighed. "Boy, I wish I could think of something she could help me with."

"Tell her you want to learn how to seduce a girl in French."

"That's too obvious."

"Tell her you want to write a love letter in French to your girl friend at home."

"Yeah, but then she'd think I have a girl friend, which I don't . . . And anyway, why would I want to write it in French if she's American?"

"Okay, okay, you said you wanted suggestions."

"I'll think of something," Alex said dreamily. "I've *got* to!"

*   *   *

Joel looked out the window of the room he was going to share with Alex. Before him was a small park circled by brick and stone houses. He had walked through it earlier, not having time to stop, just mentally drinking in the atmosphere. The trees were lovely. Were they chestnut? He had taken botany as a freshman, but retained nothing practical from it except an obscure phrase or two. In the center of the park stood a stone edifice. It was formal but simple. He remembered how his mother, who had studied art in Paris when she was young, had said, "What's different is that everything is beautiful. It makes you look at life differently. You'll never look at things the same way again."

That night they stayed up until two, talking. Joel felt glad he had made a friend so soon. It helped to have someone to talk to. And he was relieved to have met someone whose French was even worse than his!

"At least you've already got someone!" he said. He was lying on bed, in pajamas, staring at the ceiling.

"What do you mean, got someone?" Alex said.

"Well, you like her . . . She seems to sort of like you."

"Well, that's not much."

"It's something . . . You should try being *me* for a few days. You'd appreciate being you!"

"You just don't have enough self-confidence. . . . I'm not that terrific looking."

"You're tall, at least."

"Five-ten . . . That's not so tall."

"Compared to five-seven it is . . . No girl wants someone who's five-seven."

"Didn't you see that movie *Manhattan?* Woody Allen isn't that big, and that girl who liked him was around four inches taller than he was."

"Yeah, but he's Woody Allen. That's different . . . I don't know. It's probably my personality too. I mean, face it, you have to have at least one *or* the other—personality or looks."

"You have a personality! What do you mean?"

"Not the right kind, not for getting girls."

"Didn't you ever get *anyone?*

"Uh-uh . . . Not even close."

"That's too bad," Alex said sympathetically.

"There was this one girl who I think *sort* of liked me, Cathy Burridge," Joel reflected. "And one time we came back to her apartment after a movie and she said her parents were away for the weekend and her brother was sleeping and . . . well, I guess I should have done something."

"How come you didn't?"

"I don't know . . . I thought she'd get mad or something."

"Yeah, sometimes they do," Alex said.

"You know what I sometimes imagine?" Joel said.

"What?"

"Well, I go back over that scene with Cathy, only sometimes she's not Cathy, but someone really beautiful, and she says I should wait in the living room because she's going to make us some cocoa or something. So I sit there reading some magazine and all of a sudden she says, 'Here it is'—and she walks in the room naked!"

Alex sighed. "Yeah, I think of things like that too a lot. . . . I'll tell you *my* favorite one. Do you want to hear it?"

"Sure," said Joel.

"Well, I'm on some ocean liner and it starts to go under and all the passengers have to get into little boats? So I get into this little boat with this really beautiful girl that I've seen but haven't had a chance to speak to . . . And we survive some days at sea and get to sort of know each other and then we come to this island. Only the thing is, all around the island are these sort of brambles. So we try to climb through them and all our clothes, which are all kind of worn out from the rain and stuff, just get torn off."

"Then what happens?" Joel said. He had to admit it was a much better fantasy than his. It was almost like a movie!

"Well, there we are on the island, and it's this beautiful tropical climate where you don't really *need* clothes, and the thing is, she's this very shy girl who's gone to a Catholic school and really never knew much about boys, so at first she's embarrassed, even though she has a fantastic figure, but then . . . well, it all works out. I mean, we live there for six months or so, catching fish and eating wild berries and—"

"Are there any wild animals on the island?" Joel asked nervously.

"Uh-uh . . . No tigers or lions . . . Just a few monkeys and deer and that kind of thing."

"Why do you go back after six months?"

"Well, a boat comes by and we realize it's our last chance to return to civilization."

"So? If *I* saw it coming, I'd hide!"

"Yeah . . . I see your point. . . . Well, maybe it comes by after a year instead of six months."

"I like that," Joel said, bemused. "I think I saw a movie like that once. But it wasn't as good."

"Yeah, I have a visual sense," Alex said. "I'd sort of like to make movies one day . . . or maybe be a musician, I can't decide."

"I'm not at all artistic," Joel said. "Listen, was there any girl that you—I mean did you ever—"

"There was Susan," Alex said, sighing.

"Who was *she?*"

"Well, it's sort of a long story—or not so much *long* as . . . The thing is, we went to school together since we were, like, ten. And she always had sort of a crush on me. She used to ask me to help her with math. She's awful in math. So I did, and then, well, she got kind of cute looking, sort of filled-out, and when we were in high school we began dating and we just sort of began sleeping together."

"How was it?" Joel asked, trying not to be completely overwhelmed with envy.

"Okay. . . . The trouble was, I always felt like she did it to get me, you know?"

"Well, what's wrong with that?"

"Nothing, except . . . well, like with sex, she

never . . . seemed to really *like* it all that much. It was like she put up with it because she was afraid otherwise I might start liking someone else . . . which was true, in a way. Anyway, then I did this kind of dumb thing?"

"What?"

"Well, Susan had this friend, Helen, who was kind of a . . . well, a little like that girl on the bus, the dark-haired one? Kind of cute and a great figure, but knew it, used to walk around wiggling her ass at everybody. And we were in this play together our senior year, and we were lovers—in the play—and we started rehearsing and, well, you can imagine the rest."

"God, I wish things like this would happen to me!" Joel said.

"It wasn't so terrific," Alex said. "First, Susan practically had a nervous breakdown and her parents got really mad at me because her grades got so bad they thought she wouldn't be able to get into college. And Helen, well, she was—she did like sex, that's true."

"So? What more do you want?"

Alex looked pensive. "I don't know. Maybe I have a romantic soul. I just always thought it would be great if it was someone I really loved and had a lot in common with and the sex was great also."

"Yeah, well, sure," Joel said. "Only does that ever happen in real life?"

"I don't know," Alex said. "You can dream, though."

"You think that with—that woman, Madame Tessier, you could, it would be like that?"

"Yes," Alex said softly. "Well, it might be fantastic. . . . Hey, listen, we better get to sleep . . . classes start tomorrow."

"That was a good talk," Joel said.

"You'll meet somebody," Alex said. "Don't worry. Paris is the place."

"Yeah, it's the place, all right," Joel said. "But am I the person?"

3

"It's my apartment too," Melanie said heatedly. "Where are we supposed to go?"

Laura looked from her to Jean-Claude, Melanie's latest, whom she'd picked up at the Eiffel Tower two weeks earlier. "Go to *his* place," she said curtly.

"He doesn't *have* a place."

"How come? What is he—a bum?"

"I don't care *what* he is! He's great in the sack, and he likes me."

"And that's all you want?"

"Yes! Why? Just because you'd rather sit around moping and writing letters to David! That's not my idea of how to have a good year in Paris!"

Jean-Claude, who had looked bored and uncomprehending throughout this exchange, said, "I theenk I spleet now, baby. Too much hassle here, you know?"

"No!" Melanie shrieked. "Don't go! Wait a sec ... Laura, please, just this once?"

"Where should I go?"

"Joel said you could come over to his place and watch TV for a couple of hours."

"Terrific."

"Or you can read ... It's nice and quiet. He and Alex are living with this widow. Please!"

"Oh, okay," Laura said. "What's the address?"

"It's right around the corner," Melanie said eagerly. "Listen, thanks, I'll do it for you when you come to your senses and realize there's more to life than David."

Laura walked disconsolately around the corner. Madame Pimot answered the door. Laura explained she had come to study with Joel. "If that's all right?" she added anxiously.

"*Oh, mais oui*, come right in." Madame Pimot's face broke into a big smile. "He has no girl friends. I tell him: 'You are in Paris! You must live! You must love!' But he just sits reading all the time."

Laura felt it would be too complicated to explain that she and Joel had no romantic interest in each other whatsoever. "Thank you," she said politely.

"Hi," Joel said. He was wearing a sweater and corduroy slacks, now that it was almost December. "Cold out?"

"Kind of." She sat down in a chair.

"Can I bring you something?" Madame Pimot said eagerly. "Some tea? A little cognac?"

"Oh, no, thanks," Laura said. "That's awfully sweet of you, though."

"Then I will just tiptoe out and do my sewing." She closed the door behind her.

Laura and Joel smiled at each other.

"She thinks I'm your girl friend," she said sadly.

"Well . . ." said Joel.

"Where's Alex?"

"He—well, don't tell him I told you this, but he has this crush on Madame Tessier and he spends a lot of time wandering around following her."

"But she's so old! And she's married."

"Yeah, well, you never know where love will strike, I guess."

"She'd never be interested in someone like *him!*" Laura said. "He's wasting his time."

"I think he sort of knows that," Joel said, "but he has a romantic soul."

Laura sighed. "Everybody over here's in love," she said.

"I'm not," said Joel.

"Everyone but us," she said.

"You mean Melanie—"

"Oh, that's not *love.* . . . She drags in this . . . creep! Just because he's French! I mean, big deal! So what? Who says French men are such terrific lovers? David—"

"You really miss him?" Joel said sympathetically.

"Yeah, it's *awful,*" Laura said. "I know I should try and get . . . interested in other things, but I keep thinking about him *all* the time!"

"That must be love, then," Joel said. "I've never been in love, so I wouldn't know."

"Never?" Laura was surprised. She thought everyone had been in love at least once.

"Well, not so it was . . . reciprocal."

"Oh . . . That's too bad."

"Yeah." Joel looked philosophical. "Oh, it'll happen someday, I'm sure . . . when I'm eighty-five or something."

"You know what your problem is?" Laura said. "You don't have enough self-confidence."

"Everyone says that," Joel said.

"Why don't you just go up to some really pretty French girl and ask her out?"

"She'd probably laugh her head off."

"No! You're really nice-looking, Joel, in an interesting kind of way."

"I am?"

"Yes." She tried to sound more enthusiastic than she felt. "You have nice eyes and nice . . . hair. Lots of girls would like you!"

"Would *you?*" he said suddenly.

Laura was taken aback. "You mean, if it wasn't for David?"

"Yes."

"Well, I don't know. I never really thought about it. But anyway, *that* doesn't matter. I think *lots* of girls would. You just have to try."

"You're right," Joel said, suddenly looking more cheerful. "I think I'll do it."

"I mean, what can you lose?" Laura said. "So

someone turns you down? You're no worse off than you were before."

"True. . . . Anyway, rejection is probably . . . good for you," Joel said, not very convincingly. "It toughens you. . . . Of course, acceptance is probably even better."

Laura smiled. "It *is* kind of nice," she said wistfully.

They picked up their books and started to read.

*　　*　　*

"You've been enjoying yourself here?" Madame Tessier said.

"Well, yes," said Alex. "I've—uh—"

"But how about your studies! You are falling behind! And such a distinguished record at your college."

She was standing behind her desk. Her office was a small room, dominated mainly by the large, elegant desk. Unlike his own desk at home, this one was immaculately neat, with all the papers neatly arranged. An antique inkwell stood to one side and a bronze frog rested on top of a thin sheaf of newspaper clippings.

Alex cleared his throat. "Well, it's sort of on purpose," he said. "You see, I don't want to just work my head off while I'm here. I want to do what you said that first day . . . I want to immerse myself in French culture and in French . . . everything. I think I can get more walking down the street looking at the people and . . . smelling the smells than in just studying French verbs."

"There is something in what you say," Madame Tessier said. She was wearing her hair pinned up in the back. A pair of pearl earrings hung from her ears. She has beautiful ears, Alex thought, not following what she was saying. "I suffered from the same thing as a student, so I understand what you are trying to say."

"Which thing?" Alex said.

"Studying too much . . . being cut off from life."

"You did?" He was amazed.

"Yes, and now I regret it very very much. . . . You are only young once, after all!"

He stared at her. "Well, yeah, only sometimes it doesn't seem that great—being young, I mean."

She smiled. "When you are older and it is gone, then you appreciate it, the intensity, everything! . . . You have that, you have an artist's soul. I see that in you."

Alex almost fell through the floor. "Well, I do . . . I write songs."

"You must cultivate that part of yourself," she went on intensely, looking at him with her beautiful long-lashed eyes. "Perhaps this year you will find what you are searching for, those things of the spirit, of the heart."

"I hope so," Alex said softly.

"Yes, but you are bright enough to also learn up here," she said, tapping her head lightly. "You can do both. Learn about life and also study, be disciplined in your work, and do what your professors ask of you. Will you do that? For me?"

If she had asked if he would walk naked through the streets of Paris for the next month, he would have said yes, gladly. As it was, he could just stammer, "Yes, I will . . . Madame Tessier."

"Martine," she said. "My name is Martine."

"That's a . . . nice name," he said.

"I never liked it!" she said suddenly. "I always thought my sisters got the pretty names: Isabelle, Jeanne . . ."

"No, I like Martine much better," he said. "It suits you. It's very . . . musical."

She stood gazing at him, and he felt as though he were being hypnotized. "I'm glad you like it," she said softly.

I like *everything* about you, he wanted to say, but couldn't.

"Martine!" It was Monsieur Tessier, looking irritable as usual. "Aren't you finished?" he said.

"In a moment," she said coolly. "We are discussing Alex's studies."

He gave her a sardonic glance and closed the door behind him.

"You will have to excuse my husband," she said. "His manners are not always . . . He is a bit abrupt."

"How come you married him?" he found himself saying, to his horror.

Her eyes widened. "How come?"

"No, I mean, it's just you're so . . . beautiful and . . . he's so . . . awful."

She smiled with a sad expression. "It's very complicated," she said. "He was my professor. I admired him a greal deal. . . . Things change as you get to know someone better. I was very young, eighteen—I didn't know."

"I guess I feel like you deserve somebody better than that," he said, emboldened by her reply.

"That's very sweet of you," she said softly, "to say that. I don't know. You probably have an idealized portrait of me. I'm not so wonderful myself!"

"Yes, you are!" he burst out.

"Well." She looked at him. "It's nice of you to think so."

"I think you're the most beautiful woman I've ever seen," he said, amazed at his courage. His heart was beating loudly. "He must be crazy, not to realize that."

She smiled again. "Paris is full of beautiful women."

"No . . . not like you. I look at them all the time. Well." He stopped, suddenly embarrassed. "I'm sorry."

"For what?"

"For, well, criticizing your husband and—maybe I shouldn't have said some of those things."

"You should say whatever you feel," she said seriously. "Only when you are young can you do that. Afterward you learn to hide, to conceal, to lie."

Alex stared at her. *I love you!* he wanted to say, but he couldn't. "Thank you for your . . . advice," he stammered. "I'll try to do my best."

"I know you will," she said warmly. "And remember, if anything comes up, please feel free to come and talk to me."

"Yes," he said. "I will."

He walked out of the conference with her in a total daze. He wandered around the street, not having any idea where he was or where he was going. If it had been possible to shatter into small pieces due to repressed longing, he thought he would have done so immediately. He kept replaying their conversation in his mind: "You have an artistic soul." . . . "I'm glad you like it." . . . "Please feel free to come and talk to me." For her sake he would study his head off! He would get the best grades in the whole damn school! He raced home and, for two hours, sat and studied like a maniac, thinking all the time of her. *Martine.* It *was* a musical name. It was beautiful!

Finally, in the late afternoon, he went out for a break. He strolled along the Rue de la Paix. The lofty column in the center of the Place Vendôme glittered in the sun, with Napoleon perched cockily on top. He had strolled along here before, but knew from having tried a few places that the prices were out of sight for any presents for his family. Still, it was fun looking in the shop windows and imagining what he might get if he had a thousand dollars. The Place Vendôme was huge. Even at its most crowded, Alex had never seen it look anything but oversized and grand, as though it had been designed to make anyone feel slightly lost. The shops with their elegant clothes and antiques were like jewel boxes set discreetly out of sight. He gazed thoughtfully at a pearl-handled umbrella. His mother would like that. She collected umbrellas. But he knew better than to go in and ask the price. Probably it was something a family of four could live on for half a year.

Suddenly he looked up. About ten paces ahead of him was Madame Tessier—Martine—looking at something. Before he could think, she vanished inside the store. He hesitated and then walked to the store: *Joe Cowboy Jeans*. Quietly he slipped in behind some other customers. There was loud American country-and-western music blaring on some stereo speakers.

"May I help you, monsieur?" asked a salesgirl.

"Um—no, I'm just . . . looking," he said.

He looked around. Where had she gone? Then he saw her briefcase in the row of dressing stalls, on the floor. Blindly, he snatched up a shirt and went over to the dressing stall opposite hers. He stood there, peering out. A salesgirl came and swung open the door to the stall where Madame Tessier—Martine—he kept thinking of her as Madame Tessier!—was dressing. The salesgirl handed her some jeans. As she left, the doors stayed slightly ajar. Transfixed, he watched as he caught a glimpse of Madame Tessier slipping off her skirt and blouse. She stood there in her panties and bra. Alex thought he was going to faint. He stood there as quietly as possible, gazing at her in disbelief. She had a beautiful body, slim, her breasts small and delicate in the lacy bra. Jesus! he thought, leaning on the wall for support. Why didn't everyone in the store suddenly vanish! The two of them would be left alone. He would walk over to her and say . . .

The salesgirl had returned with a T-shirt. Madame Tessier started to put it on. Then, reconsidering, she pulled it off and took off her bra. One second later she pulled the T-shirt on. He was dazed. I must be going crazy, he thought. This can't be happening. Although she was in the T-shirt now, he kept remembering her as she had stood there for that one second with nothing on but her panties, her pink nipples round and soft-looking. I can't stand it, he thought. It's too much. I shouldn't have come in here.

In a T-shirt and jeans, Madame Tessier stepped out of the booth. Alex flattened himself against the wall. She approached a triple viewing mirror. As he watched, she began inspecting herself in the outfit. You look great, he thought. You look wonderful. Almost as good as you looked naked. The tight T-shirt outlined her breasts; the jeans clung to her slim hips. As he stared, she started moving to the music. She moved slowly and unself-consciously, as though she were alone, dancing by herself. Alex stared at her in fascinated amazement. Then, a moment later, she nodded to the salesgirl and ducked back into the dressing room.

He watched as she emerged, paid for the T-shirt and jeans, and left the store. Stunned, he raced out after her. She was already halfway down the block. Good. He mustn't get so close—she would see him!

She turned the corner. He followed slowly. She went over to a car parked on the sidewalk in front of a garage. The car had a protective cover over it. She set down her briefcase and pulled the cover off. Alex watched, amazed, as she uncovered a gunmetal-gray Corvette Stingray. She tossed the cover in the back, stopped to remove a leaf that had fallen on the hood—and got into the car.

The motor roared to life, echoing in the narrow street. There was a squeal of tires as the Stingray turned the corner and zoomed off down the street.

Alex went home. Joel still wasn't back. It actually *happened*, he thought, reliving the whole thing second by second. I wasn't dreaming. It *happened*. He saw her breasts again as she turned, her hips moving to the dance. Christ! What am I going to *do?* he thought. It seemed to him that never in his life had he ever wanted anything as much as he wanted her at that moment. If someone had come and said, "You can have her if you agree to start college over right from the start, take *all* your courses again," he would have done it in a second! He would have had both legs broken, anything!

He lay there, staring at the ceiling. Would it be possible to just go up to her and say, "I love you. I want to sleep with you"? After all, as Joel said, what harm could it do? But what if she got mad? What if she refused to even *speak* to him after that? She thought he was this sensitive, artistic soul, and here he was, just interested in getting her into bed. She would be totally disillusioned, horrified.

There was nothing he could do, he realized with

despair. Except daydream and follow her around and invent as many excuses as possible to go to her office. Maybe he shouldn't let his grades get *too* good. Then she wouldn't have anything to talk to him about! He closed his eyes. The room vanished. They were together in a big bed. Light was streaming in softly from the window. She was lying in his arms. "I knew you were watching me," she said. "I wanted you all along. I was just waiting for you to make the first move. I was too shy to—"

Suddenly the door opened. It was Joel. "Hi!" he said cheerfully. "Hey, guess what? Mom sent me some homemade peanut butter, the super-chunk kind! Want some?"

Alex started. He looked at him, horrified. "Peanut butter?"

"Yeah, it's great. Wait till you try it. It has a fantastic taste."

Alex sat up. He put his hand to his head. "I don't know," he said.

Joel looked at him, frowning. "What? What's wrong? You look sick."

"I *am* sick."

"Do you have fever?"

"It's worse than that."

"Is it contagious?" Joel asked nervously.

"It could be."

Alex told him about the afternoon.

"Gosh!" was all Joel could say. "You really saw her without . . . anything?"

"She had her underpants on."

"That's all?"

"Yeah."

"Wow."

"I don't know what I'm going to *do!*" Alex said desperately. "I'm not going to be able to study or concentrate on *anything*."

"You've really got it bad," Joel said sympathetically.

"You should have seen her!" Alex said.

"I wish I had," Joel said.

"Her pants started to ride up and she turned around and kind of . . . tucked them back into place. She was just . . . I don't know. I don't think she's real."

"She's real, all right."

"If only there were some—you know, some aphrodisiac, something I could—just give her and—"

"Yeah," Joel said ruefully. "That would be good."

Alex smiled. "If I could get her on that desert island."

"Sure . . . Dream on."

"Maybe I should just . . . try and do it. They say women like it when you use force."

"How would you do it?"

"Go to their house one day."

"He'd be there."

"True. . . . Maybe one day he'll go away on a trip or something."

"He probably makes her wear a chastity belt when he's gone."

Alex nodded. "If I was married to her, I would!

. . . So—what do you think. Say he did go away. Should I just, you know, appear and—"

"What do you have in mind? Sweep her off her feet?"

"I think I could. . . . She doesn't look *too* heavy. I just don't know if she'd like it."

"What's-her-name in *Gone With the Wind* liked it."

"Yeah, but I'm not Clark Gable."

"My sister says rape is a crime of violence, not sex," Joel said.

"Oh, I wouldn't rape her," Alex said hastily. "I'd only do it if she wanted. If she said to stop, I'd stop."

"Don't they sometimes say to stop when they really don't mean it?"

"Yeah, I guess you have to learn to tell the difference. . . . Oh, hell, what am I talking about? He's not going to go away, she probably has a lover already—"

"But you follow her around all the time. Wouldn't you have seen him by now if she did?"

"True," Alex said, brightening at the thought.

"I mean, even if you didn't see *him*, you'd see her going to his place or something."

"Yeah . . . But I mean, why doesn't she, if her husband is such a shit?"

Joel shrugged. "I don't know . . . Maybe the right person hasn't come along so far."

"And you think I'm the right person?"

"I didn't say *that*," Joel said. "Anyhow, it's not

whether *I* think you're the right person, it's what *she* thinks."

"True." Alex looked pensive. "Sometimes, when we're talking, she looks at me with this kind of . . . longing expression. Only maybe that's just my imagination."

"What kind of expression? I don't exactly get what you mean."

"Oh, sort of . . . wistful or sad or . . . like she wishes her life was different. I guess she must know I like her."

"That's good," Joel said, obviously trying to be encouraging.

"I guess. . . . If I were—more suave or something! I keep feeling she sets up these great lines and I don't know what to say back! I try to think of the right thing, and it comes out dumb!"

"How did she look compared to Susan?" Joel wanted to know.

"Susan?" Alex looked puzzled.

"You know. Susan, that girl you—"

"Oh . . . Oh, God, Susan! Susan was . . . well, Susan . . . I mean, Madame Tessier—her name is Martine. Isn't that a great name?"

"Yeah, it's nice," Joel said noncommittally.

"Martine . . . I can't get used to calling her Martine. Well, she just . . . Like, she had this really great underwear. Susan used to just wear Snoopy underpants and no bra. Hers was kind of lacy and—"

"Was she still in good shape? Playboy says they

won't print nude centerfolds of women over eighteen because they start sagging."

"Really?" Alex looked surprised. "No, she wasn't sagging at all! Her breasts were just . . . great. And the way she danced. You feel like she does have this playful side, only she never gets to show it with *him.*"

Joel sighed.

Alex went over and got out his books. Sitting there, he read half a line, spent ten minutes thinking of Madame Tessier, read another half a line, and thus pleasantly occupied the time until dinner.

4

"You never go anywhere without your dictionary," Alex said, as Joel set out to buy some stationery supplies.

"What if I forget the right word?"

"Make it up!"

Joel smiled and raised his eyebrows. "It's easy for you. You have a knack for languages. I don't."

"Scram! I have to study."

In the stationery store, the man at the front hardly let him get his first words out before he said, "Aha! An American! One moment!"

Shit, Joel thought. How can they tell so fast? He waited patiently as a girl showed up from the back. The man fired off some rapid French, which Joel didn't understand. He stood gazing at her. She looked vaguely familiar. Had he seen her somewhere? Her face reminded him of the face on a

Valentine his mother had given his father—very delicate, with big fawnlike eyes and a tiny nose and mouth. Her hair was short and wispy, which accentuated the delicateness.

"You wish something?" she said crisply.

Joel broke out of his trance. "Uh—yes . . . I need—*j'ai une liste.*" He took out his list and read the items he needed. When he was finished, she took the list and glanced at it.

"I speak English," she said in English.

"Oh," he said, mortified. "Well, it's true, my French isn't so good, but we're supposed to practice. We're supposed to become fluent by the end of the year. I'm here studying at the Institute for French Studies."

"Yes, I know it," the girl said. "Many of their students come here. You need paper clips? How many? A box? A carton?"

"Well—uh—how many are in a box?" Joel asked.

She climbed up on a stool to fetch a box. Joel glanced longingly up at her legs. Slender and lovely like the rest of her. She climbed down and dumped the paper clips on the table in front of him. There seemed something slightly hostile about her manner. What did I do wrong? he thought. Just being American? Speaking bad French?

"Count them," she said coolly.

Joel smiled awkwardly, hoping to get on her good side somehow, and began counting the clips. "Right—*quatre, six, huit, dix, douze.*"

At the cash register she took his money, but

didn't seem to have warmed up any. He thought desperately of Laura's and Alex's advice. But you can't ask somebody out if they consider you a total ass, he thought. I'll do it with the next one. He stood there, bemused. She disappeared into the back of the store.

Outside it was a sunny, cold day. Well, another failure. So much for that. Suddenly he saw her running after him. Had he forgotten something?

She stopped breathlessly in front of him. "I am sorry I was so rude," she said.

Joel looked at her, bewildered. "Well, you weren't—"

"Yes, I was very rude," she insisted, "and I am sorry. Here is something—a free gift from Librairie Giret. It's a handy metric converter." She slipped the card into his pocket and smiled up at him beguilingly. He felt confused.

"This is handy," he said. "I'm always getting my inches and centimeters confused. Thanks."

"And if you or any of your friends need anything at all, my name is Toni."

"Oh . . . Well, I'm Joel."

She smiled with incredible sweetness and extended her hand. Joel took it. Finally he let it go and started walking backward, still in a daze, smiling at her. "Thank you, Toni," he said softly. "Goodbye."

"Bye-bye." She smiled again. There was a mischievous glint in her eye which gleamed through impishly. Wow. He watched her trot quickly back into the store.

Alex heard Joel's account of his morning with

little sympathy. "Prettier than Madame Tessier?" he said. "I don't believe it."

"Well, in a different way," Joel qualified. "More . . . gaminlike. She had these big eyes."

"Madame Tessier has big eyes."

"She looked kind of young," Joel said. "Maybe it was her hair, really short."

"I like women with long hair," Alex said.

"Well, she looked really pretty with it short. It just kind of suited her."

They were on the roof of the institute, looking down.

"Madame Tessier—Martine—arrives here at seven in the morning," Alex said. "She leaves at about five and walks down the street where she parks her car. It's a Stingray."

"Boy, you'd make a good detective."

"There she is. She's on her way to lunch. When the weather was nice, she'd eat in the small park on Avenue Foch. Today she'll go to the café on Wagram."

They stood gazing down. Madame Tessier stopped. She looked around and started back in the direction she came.

"Now what's she doing?" Alex said.

"She probably forgot something."

They watched her approach a corner grocery and stop at the small sidewalk display.

"No, I don't think so," Alex said. "I think maybe . . . I think she's looking for me."

"What're you talking about?" Joel said. "She's

looking at the fruit stand. She's going to buy an apple."

"No, she's thinking to herself—'Where is he? He's usually following me.' She's disappointed. Where's Alex?"

"The asshole's up here on the roof staring at her. . . . Alex, you're nuts. She's not—"

They watched as Madame Tessier put an orange back on the fruit stand and walked a few steps out into the street. She looked down the street.

Joel turned to Alex with amazement. "My God, you're right. She *is* looking for you."

Madame Tessier turned and walked away again. They watched her small figure retreat down the narrow street. Joel looked at Alex. He was smiling a beatific smile.

* * *

Star Trek was on. Every evening Joel sat and watched it with Madame Pimot. She seemed to have accepted now that he had no girl friends, and although she clucked over him from time to time about going out with girls, he knew she also enjoyed his company. She had been widowed only a short time. It would have been the perfect situation for a Madame Tessier—like romance except that she was about as unsexy as possible.

Alex passed through the sitting room. Looking at Joel, he shook his head. "Hey, come in here a sec, will you?" he called a minute later.

"Wait just one minute," Joel called back. "It'll be over in a minute."

"I thought you'd seen every episode five times at least!"

"I have . . . in English. It's kind of different hearing Mr. Spock speaking in French."

Alex shook his head. In the room later he said, "What is with you? I mean it. You're like a shut-in."

"How was the concert?" Joel asked mildly, ignoring him.

"Fine. . . . The French still love jazz. Then I come back to the retirement home."

"Well, Madame Pimot hasn't been a widow long and I think she's lonely."

Alex snorted. "Not anymore, now that she's got her new adopted son who came from America to keep her company."

"I had to finish an essay for—" Joel began feebly.

"Essays! Papers!" Alex exploded. "Books all over the bed!"

"I'll clean up," Joel said hastily.

"If you want to read something," Alex said, "read this." As Joel cleared his books off Alex's bed, Alex found one of his own books. He flipped it open and stood reading: " 'If you are lucky enough to have lived in Paris as a young man, then wherever you go for the rest of your life, it stays with you, for Paris is a moveable feast.' Ernest Hemingway!" He tossed the book to Joel. "And what're you going to write in *your* memoirs?" he said sardonically. "If you've lived in Paris as a young man, you're lucky, for Paris is a great place to watch old reruns of *Star Trek*.' Joel Weber."

Joel, smiling, sat listening to Alex's onslaught resignedly. He turned over one of his spiral notebooks and glanced down at it.

"You're like a mole!" Alex said. "All you've seen of Paris is the subway to the institute! You've got to get out of here—do something!"

"You're right," Joel said.

"You always say I'm right and then you don't *do* anything."

"Listen, tomorrow I'm calling up a French girl I met and I'm going to ask her out."

"Really?"

"Yup."

"Okay, terrific. I'll believe it when it happens."

"You'll see," Joel said. "Just wait."

*　　*　　*

The phone rang twice before someone picked it up. Joel heard a soft feminine voice say, "*Librairie Giret, oui? . . .* What? Just a moment." Then another voice came on. "Hello, yes?

He was calling from the institute's lounge and could hardly hear above the music playing in the background. "Toni?" he said quickly. "Hi, this is Joel. I've been by the shop a couple of times buying things. Remember me?"

"Yes," she said, "I remember you, but—"

"Well, I just wondered if you weren't busy Saturday night? I thought maybe you'd like to see a movie or go to dinner."

"Saturday night?" She seemed to hesitate a second. His heart sank. "Well, okay, Saturday is good."

"Okay, then?" he said, elated. "Great. Well, listen, where do you live? What's your address." He thought he could hear laughter in the background. "What's so funny?"

"Nothing . . . I'm just so happy about Saturday. Here's my address—are you ready? Number 138, Avenue de Wagram, Paris 17. Okay?"

"Right, got it. I'll see you Saturday then, about eight o'clock. Okay, 'bye."

Alex was sitting nearby, reading. "Hey, I did it!" Joel said. "And she said yes!"

"What did I tell you?"

"It was easy! I just asked and—"

"You're on your way, pal . . . Seducing her will be child's play after this."

"Seducing her?" Joel looked horrified. "On the first date?"

Alex grinned. "Sure . . . Just think up a couple of good lines."

"I don't know any."

"Invent some . . . You've got till Saturday."

"She's not that type," Joel said hastily.

"Oh?" Alex looked skeptical. "What type is she?"

"Well, she seems . . . She's very delicate looking, like I said. . . . She may not have gone out with boys that much."

Alex kept looking at him with the same expression.

"Will you cut it out?" Joel said, mad. "You've never even *met* her! You just think all French girls are ready to jump into bed with every American they meet."

"Did I say that? . . . I just think she may have had a little more experience than you're giving her credit for."

Joel shook his head emphatically. "She's a real old-fashioned girl," he said. "My mother would like her."

"Those are the kind to look out for," Alex said.

Joel shook his head. "You're impossible."

Later that day he saw Laura at the Café Flore. She sat there every day waiting for Sartre and Simone de Beauvoir to appear and have a drink together. She was almost as bad as Alex with Madame Tessier!

"Have they come yet?" he said.

"Not yet. . . . Thursdays they're often late," she said. "So, how goes it?"

"Listen, I did it!" he said excitedly, sitting down next to her. "I asked her out, that girl I told you about."

Laura smiled. She had a lovely, warm smile. "That's great, Joel. I'm really proud of you."

"Yeah, I feel good . . . It wasn't that hard."

"You'll see . . . I bet she'll really like you."

"Alex got me so mad," he said. "He thinks just because she's French she's going to go to bed with any American that asks her."

"Well," Laura said judiciously. "Some of them are like that."

"*She's* not," he said earnestly. "She's not that type. She has a very . . . sweet manner, sort of shy almost. Only there's like a little gleam in her eyes at the same time."

Laura smiled. "God, men are so easy to fool!" she said.

Joel was startled. "What do you mean?"

"You fall for anything! It's sad . . . but sweet, I guess, in a way."

Joel's heart began beating rapidly. "What am I falling for? She really *is* like that."

Laura just smiled enigmatically. "You'll find out what she's like, but believe me, she'll be a lot different from all these little illusions you've concocted about her."

"You sound just like Alex," he said, hurt. "How do you know they're illusions?"

"Take it from me," Laura said. "They are. . . . Listen, I do it too. We all do. We figure out what illusion you want and we act it out. I did it with David. We were taking this Romantic Poetry class together and I knew he was the romantic type, so I'd come to class with my hair loose, in these soft, flowing blouses, with a kind of dreamy, Botticelli-like expression . . . It worked." She grinned.

"Well, but is that so bad?" Joel said.

"Yeah, in a way . . . I bet *she* doesn't do that with *him*."

"Who? With who?"

"De Beauvoir with Sartre . . . See, that's the

64

kind of relationship I admire. Totally equal. She does her thing, he does his. They've never even lived together. They just meet every day. It's all so . . . civilized."

"It sounds a little bloodless to me," Joel said.

"It isn't!" Laura insisted. "It's the perfect relationship . . . The only trouble is, I think it was based partly on their not having kids. I mean, the whole separate-apartment bit . . . And I kind of think I'd like kids. And if I had them, I'd want whoever was their father to pitch in and, you know, help with everything. That's where the trouble begins."

"Why trouble?" Joel wanted to know.

"No, I don't mean trouble . . . But it stops being so . . . perfect . . . And then the other thing, which I think is great in theory, is this thing they had where they both had affairs with other people and were totally open about it. I just don't know how I'd feel if David—"

"That never works," Joel said.

"How do you know?" Laura said.

"People get jealous," he said. "It's human nature."

"But look at *them!*" Laura said. "They're still together after fifty *years!* . . . Oh look, there they are! Isn't it sweet! You know, his eyesight is terrible now, he's almost blind, and she reads to him at night. They're reading this long Chinese novel aloud. I read that somewhere."

Joel sighed. He watched as the famous elderly couple sat down in their accustomed place. But all

65

he could think of, as Laura gazed at them, beaming, was Toni. He imagined her as she had looked when she ran after him outside the store, the way she had gazed up at him so sweetly. Was it all an act? Impossible! Well, who cared? She had said yes, that was all that mattered. She wanted to see him again. Now if he could only wait till Saturday!

5

Joel stood just inside the door of Toni's apartment sinking in waves of humiliation. Toni was laughing as she said, "When you called the store, you must have talked to Malsy or Cecile. I'm sure of it. I don't come in Thursday . . . But you thought it was me? That was unkind of them. They must have been teasing you, pretending to be me."

"Well," Joel said, discouraged, "it sounded like you, but it's true, there was a lot of noise in the background."

"You thought we had a date tonight?"

He nodded miserably.

"But I already have a date! I don't need two!" She pointed to a dapper-looking French guy who was lounging against a bookcase, smiling snidely at Joel.

Joel sighed. "Okay, well. I get the picture. That's

okay." He smiled wryly. "I'll just go home and shoot myself or something." He started toward the door.

Toni came running after him. "No, don't go," she said. "I have an idea. Come with us! It will give you a chance to see some sights. We'll go to a disco, we can dance. What do you say?"

She was looking up at him with that expression that had beguiled him so outside the store. "Well, won't your friend mind?" he said.

"Pascal? No! Anyway, who cares? *I* want you to come. Will you?"

Joel's heart started thumping rapidly. "Okay. sure," he said finally.

She smiled at him radiantly. "I'm so glad," she said. "You'll have a good time! You'll see!"

The bar they went to was loud and crowded. Joel found himself slammed next to Toni. Pascal was on her other side, kissing her neck. Occasionally she would swat his hand away as though he were an insect that was irritating her.

"Is this what a bar would be like in America?" she asked.

"I don't know," Joel confessed.

"But I thought you said you go to school in New York."

"I do . . . only I don't . . . go to bars that much."

She nodded. "You study all the time?"

He sighed. "I'm afraid so."

"My brother Louis is like that. It's a certain type."

Joel watched in horrified fascination as Pascal's hand reached up, caressing her breast. What was going on? Was this her boyfriend? If so, she certainly had shitty taste in men. And why was she doing this? Did she enjoy tormenting people? Was she just a bitch who liked leading men on for some kind of sadistic enjoyment? Was Laura right?

"I—maybe I better go home now," he said suddenly, not sure he could take any more.

"Goodbye," Pascal said cheerfully, obviously glad to get rid of him.

"No, don't go," Toni said in a soft, pleading voice. She put her hand on his. "We're going to have dinner with some friends at a good place. Come with us, okay? You'll like it."

In the restaurant it was the same thing. Pascal kept baiting him, rattling away in French he couldn't understand while everyone laughed at his feeble attempts to follow the conversation. Suddenly Pascal grabbed Toni's arm. A glass of wine spilled into Joel's lap. Toni looked concerned. She began patting him with her napkin. He looked at her, even more bewildered than before. Did she like him? Hate him?

"Listen, let me pay for my share," he said, "and then I'll just—get out of here."

"We're all leaving," Toni said. She turned to Pascal. "*You* pay for it!" she said heatedly. "He's our guest!" Then she turned to Joel again. "We're going to a great disco. You like to dance?"

"Yes," said Joel hesitantly.

"Good! You'll have fun. You'll like it," she predicted confidently.

The disco was even noisier than the bar and the restaurant. A laser beam and Sli-Scan light show flashed, flaring around him.

Joel tried to talk to Toni above the din. "I'm majoring in political science," he said, "and I thought knowing French would help with international relations."

"Remember Vietnam?" Pascal said sneeringly. "Ho Chi Minh shit on you."

"Hush!" Toni said. To Joel she said, "I'm studying American literature at the Sorbonne."

"Who do you study?" Joel asked. "Hawthorne? Melville?"

"Oh no, contemporary literature," she said. "Joan Didion, Philip Roth . . . You know this book *Portnoy's Complaint?*"

He nodded.

"It's very interesting. You're Jewish? Is it typical? He is a typical New York Jew?"

"Well, in a way," Joel said. "I think—"

"You defend what happened in Cuba?" Pascal broke in. "The embargo on Cuba? Watergate? Racism?"

"Pascal, shut *up!*" Toni said, to Joel's delight. "You're boring!"

"Do you want to dance?" Joel asked her, ignoring him.

"The only dancing *you* do," Pascal said, "will be the Chinese dancing on your capitalist graves!"

"You know how to dance?" Toni said, as though surprised.

"Well . . . yeah," Joel said, relieved he did.

"America *stinks*, you turkey!" Pascal yelled. He sat back, obviously loving his own joke. Joel smiled and with his foot gave Pascal's chair a little shove. Pascal fell over backward and crashed to the floor. Joel looked down at him. "Sorry about that," he said. It was, unequivocally, one of the great moments of his life. He glanced at Toni. She laughed conspiratorially and moved with him onto the dance floor.

"Don't pay any attention to Pascal," she said. "He just became a Communist."

"He certainly dresses well for a Communist," Joel said.

"He works in a men's store and gets a discount."

They began dancing. Joel had learned to dance from his sister. He was better than people expected him to be. Toni danced charmingly, moving her small, lithe body to and fro, smiling at him with that impish, charming expression. He started falling in love with her again. He forgave her everything.

Back at her apartment, he trailed along behind her and Pascal. "Well, I guess I'll be going now," he said. "Thanks for the wonderful—"

"One moment," Toni said. To Pascal she said, "Here . . . Open the door for me."

While he was fumbling with the lock, she leaned over toward Joel. "Come back in ten minutes," she whispered in his ear.

Stunned, he nodded. She smiled at him mischievously.

For ten minutes he waited in a dark corner of the street. Finally he saw Pascal emerge and get into his car. Slowly Joel climbed the steps to the apartment. Toni let him in. She smiled. "Well, finally! He is gone!"

"I guess I don't get it," Joel said. "Is he your boyfriend or not?"

She shook her head. "He used to be. . . . He got to be a pest."

"Then why do you let him paw at you that way?" he said.

Her eyes widened. "That's not important," she said blithely.

"Well, where I come from, a girl wouldn't let a boy do that unless she really liked him."

"Oh?" She looked as though the mores of the people he knew were of no importance to her whatever. "I am sorry, though. You thought I was teasing you? That was bad. I *am* bad with men sometimes." She smiled. "I like to flirt. I apologize."

"That's okay," he said. "I just couldn't tell . . . what was going on. Like in the store that day. First you acted so nasty, then all of a sudden you were very nice."

"Yes, it's true," she admitted. "It's just that so many Americans—they come here and act so . . . awful. So sure of themselves, as though they own the world."

"I'm not like that, I don't think," Joel said.

"No," she said. "Now I see that. But at first I just took you for another typical American."

"That's what Laura said," he said.

"Who is Laura?"

"Oh, she's this girl I'm friendly with, an American girl."

"You are lovers?" she asked with interest.

Joel blushed. "No, not at all! We're just friends."

"I see! American girls are like that, I've heard. They like to be friends with men. We are not so . . . we are different."

"Yes, well . . ."

"We value our femininity," she said. "We are not so into this women's-lib thing, you know?"

"Well, you are very . . . feminine," he said, wishing he could express himself with greater ease. "You have an exquisite face."

"Exquisite?" She smiled. "That is such a nice compliment. I like that! Thank you!"

"It's true," he said, blushing again. There was a silence. He stared at her, wanting to kiss her, but not knowing how to do it.

"You were so nice after that mistaken phone call," Toni said. "After a mean joke like that, anybody else would just have left."

"I know. I was going to, several times. That's a problem I have. Indecisiveness."

She frowned. "Indecisiveness?" she said. "What does that mean?"

"It means you can't make a decision," he said. "You're afraid to do things." Like kiss you. Finally,

73

in a burst of courage, he took her hand, which was lying on the table. He looked up at her desperately.

"It's very late," she said softly.

"Oh . . . right. I'm sorry." He let go of her hand and got up. They moved to the door. Finally he leaned over and kissed her. Her lips were unbelievably soft and warm. "Will I see you again?" he asked.

She smiled. "Yes, I think so."

Joel opened the door to go out. Then he realized he had made a mistake. He had walked into the bedroom. "I'm sorry," he said in confusion. "Wrong door."

"No, right door," she said. She brushed past him and went into the bedroom. She turned on a small lamp near the bed.

Joel stared at her. He couldn't tell if she was teasing him again.

"Don't you want to see if my body is as exquisite as my face?" she asked.

"Uh . . . sure," he said, still unable to do anything but stand and stare at her.

With a few quick, deft movements she removed all her clothes. Then she leapt up on the bed and got into the pose of a statue. "There! What do you think?"

He looked at her, transfixed. She had a small, delicately built body with pointed breasts and slim hips. She looked to him like some wood nymph that had slipped in from a forest glade.

"Don't you want to take something off too?" she said. "It will be easier. Here, let me help you." She jumped off the bed and went over to where he stood. She began unbuttoning his shirt. Her small fingers moved deftly. "There!" She looked up at him. "Do you want to do the rest?"

He bent down and, as though mesmerized, took her by the shoulders and kissed her. This time her mouth opened and her tongue darted into his. He let his hand wander down her back, toward her hips. Then suddenly he stopped and pulled off the rest of his clothes. She was lying in bed, waiting for him.

"You see, I'm not so bad," she said with that teasing smile.

"No, I didn't—" he began, but she put her arms around his neck.

"Kiss me again," she said.

This isn't happening, he kept thinking. I'm just imagining it. Her body moved soft, light in his arms. Her hands caressed his body. She pressed against him as though she wanted to melt into him. When he entered her, it was as though someone took him by the scruff of the neck and threw him headlong over a waterfall. All his thoughts and reasonings and analyses vanished and he was somewhere else where none of that mattered at all.

When he came to again, she was lying in his arms, snuggled against him. "So?" she said. "Was I as good as American girls?"

Joel sighed. "Well, actually . . . I never— This is the first time I ever—"

Toni looked at him in amazement. "Really? No!"

"Yes, I'm afraid so."

"But, I don't understand. Why not?"

"I guess I'm sort of shy," he confessed.

"Yes, but you mean no girl seduced you ever? How strange."

"I never thought of it that way before," he said.

"I knew you would be a good lover," she said, sighing contentedly. "Right away. You can always tell by a man's hands."

"You can?"

"Yes . . . My sister taught me that. It's always true. You have very sensitive hands. That means you are sensitive to a woman's needs, you know how to go into their soul."

Joel swallowed. "Well," he said.

"Do you forgive me for before?" she said.

"Sure," he said. "I was never mad at you anyway . . . just confused."

"I was teasing you with Pascal," she admitted. "Making you jealous. I'm sorry."

"Well, you succeeded," he admitted, "—in making me jealous, that is."

"That was unkind," she said. "Can you stay? All night?"

"Sure, I guess so," he said, imagining how amazed Alex would be.

"The first time is never so good," she said. "You have to get to know the other person's body, you know? What it can do, what it likes . . . Tell me, what do you like?"

"What do you mean?" he said.

"What do you want me to do? You know! Just tell me."

"I think I would like anything," he admitted.

"Okay," she said cheerfully. "If you don't like what I do, you tell me, all right?"

"Okay." He lay back as she began kissing him lightly all over his body. I must have died and gone to heaven, he thought. Something like that.

*   *   *

In the morning she was still there. He woke up and glanced over at her, sleeping sweetly, curled to one side, her arm dangling over the edge of the bed. He was glad he had woken up first. He lay there with a kind of almost religious awe. Everything in the room seemed magical and glowing, every object he looked at somehow transformed. It happened, he thought. I didn't imagine it. It *really* happened! But why? He thought of all those years of trying feebly and totally ineffectively to score with girls, reading articles and books on how to act, consulting with friends on what "worked." And here for some reason this beautiful girl, who obviously had her choice of all kinds of men of all ages and sizes and types, had chosen *him!* Because he had nice hands! He looked down at his hands. They looked the same to him—nothing special. Who knew why she had picked him? Maybe she didn't know either. Maybe she said that about his hands because everyone needed a "reason," no matter how foolish. He hadn't had to seduce her or flatter her or do anything! My God! And he was slightly terrified that she'd wake up and look at him and the magic that had made her act the way she had the night before would have vanished and she would wonder why she had done it.

He sighed. It *had* happened. Memories of it drifted inexorably through his mind, the way she wrapped her legs around him, like a child climbing a tree; the way she cried out, breathlessly, "Oh!" as she came, almost in surprise; the way she had said, after the second time, "No, stay in me, it feels so nice, I like it"; the way she had snuggled against him so guilelessly, her soft hair brushing against his skin. Jesus! What if she *did* change her mind? What if she *did* wake up and decide she never wanted to see him again? It didn't matter. What had happened last night was enough.

She turned over and murmured something indistinguishable, then slowly opened her eyes. Upon seeing him, she didn't recoil in horror or surprise, but just smiled, as though finding him there was the nicest possible present she could receive. "Have you been awake long?" she asked.

"Just a little," he said.

She gazed at him pensively. "Are you surprised—at being here?"

"Yes," he admitted.

"You know," she said, "I didn't want to tell you, but yesterday was my birthday. I was twenty. So you were my birthday present to myself."

He smiled.

"I like to do that," she said, "get myself something, because I always feel I know what I want better than anyone else."

"I wish I had known," he said. "I would have liked to give you something."

"You did."

He leaned over impulsively and kissed her. Immediately she put her arms around him and kissed him back, with an ardor he found amazing so early in the morning.

"Do you want to?" she said, "Or don't you like to before breakfast?"

"I—yes," he stammered, already aroused.

"Let me wash up a minute," she said, and vanished into the bathroom. She moved so quickly, like a deer! A second later she was back, cool and fresh and smelling of some wonderful scent like roses or honeysuckle. He thought if he inhaled deeply he might pass out.

"You don't mind?" she said, "that I like being with you, doing this?"

"Mind?" he said. "How could I?"

"Oh, I thought Americans . . . You know, you hear they want women to be virginal. It offends their masculinity or something to have a woman who likes to make love."

"It doesn't offend *me*," he said shyly.

"Good."

Doing it in the sunny room, being able to see her, was different, in a way less magical than the night before, when the semidarkness had cast a kind of spell on everything, but more magical in the sense that seeing her was like another aphrodisiac. She kept her eyes closed—her lashes were so long! but once she opened them, right in the middle, and he thought he would never forget that wide-eyed, soft expression as she gazed up at him.

"It's so good," she said afterward. "You make me feel so good."

"You make *me* feel very good too," he said awkwardly, wishing he could somehow express to her how she made him feel.

"I feel like you really like me," she said.

He smiled, surprised. "I do."

"No, but so many men don't really like women," she said. "They fuck like machines. It's not nice."

He didn't want to ask or even know how many men she had been with. Obviously a fair number. He preferred not to think of it.

"Do your parents love each other—this way?" she asked.

"My parents?" Joel thought. His parents were affectionate with each other. They kissed and hugged, but he had never stopped to think about what went on when they were alone together at night. "I think they do," he said.

"My father has a mistress," Toni said. "I know her. She works at the bakery on our street. She is not so young, about my mother's age, and not so pretty, but she has a certain—she sparkles? You can say that?"

"Yes," he said. "Like you."

"Do I?" she said, pleased.

"How do you know about it?" he asked.

"He told me. We are very close . . . He said I

must never tell my mother. I never will. But you think your father doesn't have a girl friend?"

"I can't imagine it." He recalled how once a babysitter had gotten a crush on his father, and his mother had gotten mad and started yelling about it. "I don't think he would do something like that."

"Why not?"

He was surprised at her surprise. "Well, I mean, maybe it's different in America. Men just don't—"

"Really? They don't have girl friends?"

"Well, I guess some do," he admitted. "But not men like my father. He's more—well, a family man . . . I would be like that," he found himself admitting.

"Really? But you can't tell . . . Say your wife is forty and you meet someone young and appealing and she says she adores you."

"It wouldn't matter," he insisted. "I'm not like that. I feel if you form a bond with someone, it's like a sacred trust."

"Oh?" She looked amazed. "You are religious?"

"No, not really. It's just—" He found it hard to explain what he meant. "I guess I would want that from another person too," he said.

"And you would never forgive if they broke that trust?"

He considered. "It would be . . . terribly painful."

She looked pensive. "You take things very seriously," she concluded.

"Yes," he admitted. "Don't you?"

"No," she said candidly. "Not that way. I want to be happy, so I do what makes me happy."

He knew that, and knew that was why she was there, but it pained him to think that if she met someone who would make her happier than he did, she would move on so carelessly. "I hope I can make you happy," he said.

She smiled at him. "You do. . . . Everything you do makes me happy. Do I make *you* happy?"

"Yes, very."

She began kissing him again on his stomach. "Does *that* make you happy?" she said mischievously.

He laughed. "If you're not careful, I'll *die* of happiness . . . How would you explain that to the police."

"I'll take my chance."

At eleven she suddenly leapt out of bed. "My goodness! I have to hurry!"

"What?" he said, startled, as she pulled on her clothes with her usual lightning speed.

"We have a concert at one!"

"Who? Who is we?"

"I didn't tell you . . . That is my . . . profession. I play the flute, and my friends, we have formed a small orchestra, a chamber orchestra. We play at people's homes, wherever. This is for a formal party."

"*I* used to play the flute," he said, delighted at the coincidence.

"Yes?" She looked delighted too. "Well?"

"Passably . . . Not to do it professionally. I stopped taking lessons when I was fifteen."

"I am very good," she said. "I think I can make it. Maybe not as a soloist, but as a member of a group, yes."

"I'd love to hear you play," he said. He could imagine her perfectly, like a wood nymph playing the flute, curled up on a rock. It was a perfect instrument for her. Had she chosen it for that reason?

"You will, someday. But today I cannot invite you. You understand?"

"Of course."

"Alphonse is nervous because he feels their harpsichord is not quite adequate. He is *always* nervous!"

"My father plays the harpsichord," Joel said. "He makes them, actually."

"Makes them?"

"Yes, in America you can get a kit, and he likes to do that. He's made three so far. Sometimes friends commission them, and he gives them away if they pay for the cost of the parts."

"How strange!" Toni said. "I didn't know Americans . . . Well, perhaps that is a stereotype. I was going to say, I didn't know they were cultured in that way. I thought they only liked rock music."

"Well, my parents probably aren't typical. They go crazy when my sister plays rock on her stereo. My mother says it's all total garbage."

"Joel? I have to run now . . . Can you let yourself out? The door locks automatically. I'm sorry, to have to rush."

"That's okay," he said.

"We will speak tonight," she said. She went over and kissed him. "Goodbye! *Au revoir!*"

"*Au revoir!*" he said softly.

*　　*　　*

After Toni had left, Joel lay there half dozing, half daydreaming, until past noon. Then he got up and showered and left the apartment. He wandered in a complete daze. It was a cold, sparkling, sunny day. Had there ever been such a lovely day before ever in the history of the world? He doubted it.

He wandered along the Boulevard Saint-Michel with its long walkway, lined with trees. One day he and Toni would go to the Luxembourg Gardens together, his favorite place in Paris so far. He loved the peaceful atmosphere of the pool with the Medici Fountain at one end, the stretches of flowers and lawns. For weeks he had wandered around, watching students strolling hand in hand, their arms around each other. Now he would be one of them!

"Hey! Joel!" It was Laura. She was sitting at the Café Flore, writing postcards to David as usual.

"Oh, hi!" he said. He went over and sat down next to her.

"You look like someone just hit you on the head with a rock."

He sighed. "Well . . ."

"What happened with that girl? Did you go out with her?"

He gave her a condensed version of what happened.

Laura sighed. "Oh God! I can't stand it! You too! Shit! It's not fair . . . No, I'm sorry. That's great. She sounds really nice."

"Maybe you should," he suggested tentatively. "I mean, since David isn't here, why don't you . . . You wouldn't have to tell him."

Laura looked at him, horrified. "You mean, just pick someone up and fuck just because I feel horny?"

"Well." He was always taken aback by her bluntness. "I just thought if there was someone you liked."

She sighed. "Oh, there are all these Frenchmen that make remarks at me. There's this one. He comes here and always tries to pick me up. He's kind of cute."

"So, why don't you—"

"But what a thing to do to David!"

"Well . . . Maybe he's feeling the same way."

"Horny? Well, sure, but he'd never . . . I mean, he's not the type to just find someone and drag her into bed."

"Sure," he said, hoping she was right.

"It wasn't just sex between us," she explained earnestly. "It was really love. I mean, it wasn't like you and this—"

"Toni . . . But *we're* in love," he said. "*I'm* in love."

"Well." Laura looked at him condescendingly. "You *think* it's love . . . It's just hormones."

Joel felt indignant. "It's not! I *love* her! She's wonderful."

Laura smiled. "Joel, you're just a *total* pushover. I knew any girl that got you into bed would have a complete marshmallow on their hands."

"Am I a complete marshmallow?" he said wryly.

"Sure! Look at you! You fuck a couple of times and you're ready to follow her to the ends of the earth."

"Well, okay, maybe I'm a little—"

"Just look out, that's all," Laura said. "She probably has a dozen French guys she's sleeping with, and decided to have a little extra fun with an American."

Joel felt as though he'd been stabbed to the heart. "I don't think so," he said stiffly.

"Listen, I'm telling you for your own good . . . She's going to murder you. You're too naïve."

"I don't think you're right," he said miserably, sure she *was* right.

"Look, let's face it," Laura said. "Anyone who hops into bed with a guy after a first date isn't exactly a virgin."

"No, I know that," he said hastily.

"She likes sex and for some reason she likes you. Great. Enjoy it while it lasts."

Joel felt in horrible pain. "I can't," he blurted. "I can't think of it that way."

Laura looked concerned. "Oh, dear . . . You mean, you want to think it's love on *her* part too?"

He nodded miserably.

"Maybe it is," Laura said. "I mean, I could be wrong. I hope it is, Joel. Really."

"She was so—" He tried to explain what it had been like, but couldn't.

"Sure." But it was clear by now that Laura felt sorry for him and was trying to comfort him. "No, listen, I just have all these probably totally unfounded prejudices about French girls. She's probably very sweet and very . . ." She trailed off, obviously unable to complete a sentence she didn't believe in.

Joel wandered home. His mood had changed totally. If only he hadn't met Laura! If only she weren't so blunt! Could she be right? That Toni was just fooling around? No, it couldn't be. She *couldn't* act that way with everyone. It just wasn't possible.

6

Laura turned the corner. She and Melanie had been wandering through the dark, bizarre labyrinth of the Grévin wax museum. They were sharing a tape-recorded tour. Laura turned to go one way, Melanie another. When Laura pulled on the tape recorder, Melanie's earplug was pulled out. She grabbed her ear. "Jesus, you nearly ripped my ear off!"

"Well, if you'd *follow* me," Laura said, annoyed.

"Follow you!" Melanie exploded. "Three museums today, God knows how many cathedrals last week! Don't you think this is becoming an obsession?"

"I've got a lot of things to see," Laura said stiffly.

"Well, I hope you enjoy them," Melanie said, "but *I've* got to get ready to go out tonight."

"With who? François? Or was he just last week's number?" Laura said sarcastically.

Melanie raised her eyebrows. "Hey, cut it out, okay? I'm here to have *fun,* to meet people, to *get* something out of my year in Paris, not to go moping around after some slob who's probably making it with another girl this very second."

"He is *not!*" Laura said furiously.

"Wanna bet? I bet you weren't two days on the plane before he—"

Laura's cheeks were blazing pink. "You don't know David!"

"I do *so!* He sounds like a total drip, if you want my opinion. Those yucky dumb letters he writes."

"How dare you read my letters!" Laura said.

"I just wanted to see if he was as big a drip as you made him sound. Well, he's even *worse!* All that garbage about 'I will be true to you forever.' God, I've never heard such *total total* shit."

"Just because *you* never met anyone who'd be faithful to you," Laura said.

"You're just using him," Melanie said. "He's like some stuffed animal you can lug around. Great! Do it! Wreck your whole year here! *I* don't care. But don't expect me to spoil *my* fun for *you.*"

"I don't," Laura said stiffly.

After Melanie had left, she sat down and tried to write David a postcard.

Dear David,
    The wax museum is really incredible. I wish so much you were here with me. I know you'd

love it. I tried taking Melanie, but she's just a *total* boor. She has no appreciation of culture at all! I simply can't stand her! I wish so much they had let me room alone. It's cold here and the weather is lousy and depressing. The whole year seems screwed up. I wish I'd stayed home.

She had run out of room. She put the postcard in her bag. And Joel finding someone! That was the last straw. She had thought she could at least count on *him* to be miserable and lonely all year with her. Just because some dopey little French girl snapped her fingers! Were men *all* that dumb? Was Melanie right about David? She remembered his last letter. He said he had gone to the movies with Tracy. He wouldn't do it with Tracy! Would he? Tracy was just as tall as he was and a terrific tennis player. She could give him a good game in singles, as Laura couldn't. But he claimed he just thought of her as a healthy, athletic type, a friend. . . . "Oh yeah?" she could hear Melanie saying. Some friend. She saw them mentally, playing tennis together. David was a good athlete. He looked sexy in his tennis shorts and T-shirt. He played indoors all winter. He would invite Tracy to play. Afterward they would go back to his place, shower together. Laura saw them standing in the shower as she and David used to. He was soaping her breasts . . .

Cut it out! That's just *sheer* masochism, she warned herself. She sighed. Oh, maybe Joel was right. Just go up to that guy who kept trailing her in the café and say, "Hi, here I am." He was cute. What harm would it do? But she couldn't. Not after David. Not after love. Just to pop into bed with someone for sex? No, I'm not the type, she decided mournfully. It's okay for Melanie with her Lover of the Week. I'm too . . . sensitive. I'm like Joel. It has to mean something. It has to be someone I *like*. Anyway, what's wrong with masturbating? There's nothing *wrong* with it, she answered herself, it's just not much fun. Fun! It was *dull!* She hated it. Before David, she had sort of enjoyed it, but now she missed the feeling of his body, the warmth, the closeness. Just to come like that, with a pillow between your legs. What was the point?

She began thinking of Simone de Beauvoir, as she often did. What did you do when Sartre found someone? she wondered. Did you masturbate? Did you cry? Didn't you care? She had said in an interview that she did care. "I never knew if I was indispensable to him," she'd said. "But he knew *he* was indispensable to me." Damn, were women *always* insecure? Even *her?*

Laura began thinking of the American boys at the institute. Maybe if I could find someone I liked, not was madly in love with, and I could just suggest we do it, in a friendly kind of way. Who? Joel was taken. Alex? She mused about Alex. She liked his looks. He reminded her slightly of David. But he had this thing about Madame Tessier. Still, that would never amount to anything. Maybe she should just say to him, "Alex, meanwhile, why don't we?"

How would he feel? Did he like her, even, in that way? Who knew?

She decided she didn't quite have the . . . courage or whatever, just to say, "Hi! Here I am" to Alex. And he had no idea she'd be interested. The usual stalemate. She could try telling Joel and *he* could tell him. Maybe that would work. "Tell Alex if he ever feels like . . ." But then what? Could she? Could she *enjoy* it even, knowing she was betraying David? What if Melanie was wrong and he'd remained faithful? And then what if she *did* enjoy it? That would be even worse! Bad if it was awful and worse if it was good.

"Hi, Laura!"

She looked up. She couldn't believe it. It was Alex. She felt very uncomfortable, as though by looking at her he might be able to read what had been in her mind.

"What are you doing here?"

"Well, I—I was going through with Melanie and I—she had to leave."

He came over and sat down next to her. "I had some time to kill," he said. "I wrote this song and I'm going to sing it to Madame Tessier."

"Oh," Laura said, disappointed. "You've still got a crush on her?"

He smiled ruefully. "Yeah, in the worst way. . . . It's kind of hopeless, basically. Joel keeps saying I should forget about her and find someone—you know, the way he did."

"I know!" Laura exclaimed. "Wasn't that amazing? I'm so pleased—for him."

93

"Me too," Alex said, "though it's a little . . . I mean, if you don't have anyone, it's kind of hard listening to someone mooning away about their terrific sex life."

"Yeah," Laura said. She was starting to feel more relaxed. "Listen, you think *you* have it bad? Melanie drags in some new guy every *week* practically!"

"You still—I guess you're still in love with that guy at home?" he asked.

She nodded. "Yeah, but it's—I mean, I feel like I'm spending my whole year just writing him postcards! . . . Melanie thinks he's probably shacking up with someone else right now."

"Well," Alex said.

"What does that mean?" Laura said quickly. "Do *you* too?"

"I don't know him," Alex said, taken aback. "How can I—"

"No, but do you think it's impossible in the abstract for a boy to be faithful to his girl friend?"

"Not impossible," Alex said slowly.

"But hard? Unlikely? Is *that* what you're trying to say?"

Alex sighed. "Well . . ."

Laura shook her head. "You too! Well, maybe I'm naïve or something. It's true, he is good looking and girls like him, but . . . would he really write all these letters saying he'd be true to me forever when he's screwing someone on the side? Could he really be *that* hypocritical?"

"Well," Alex said thoughtfully, "he may not really *like* them. He may be doing it, you know——"

"For sex?" Laura said. "Just for that?"

"Well, yeah."

"I just *hate* that!" she exploded. "I mean, I hate that whole concept, that for men it's this divided thing—they can just screw without its meaning anything."

"Look at Melanie."

"You mean girls are just as bad?"

"Some of them."

She thought about this. "Yeah, well . . . I guess it *is* a matter of personality. I think I'm more like Joel; it would have to mean something." Somewhere along the way she had realized she wouldn't have an affair with Alex, and so she felt at ease talking to him again.

Alex smiled. "That's nice, that you're like that."

"What's nice about it?" she said defensively.

"I don't know . . . It seems nicer than just jumping into bed with a dozen guys just out of sheer horniness or something, like Melanie."

"Maybe . . . She may just be more practical than me. I mean, here I am! Paris! The city of romance! And I sit here writing postcards! I bet I've written David five hundred postcards by now. Melanie is totally fed up with me. She says I'm acting like a recluse."

"Well, that is bad, maybe," Alex said. "You shouldn't overdo it."

"Oh, that's just my personality," Laura said. "I overdo *everything* . . . You know, maybe I overdid

95

the thing with David too. I saw him, I fell madly in love . . . I just overdo *everything!*"

"That's not bad," he said.

"Yes, it is," Laura said. "Why can't I be cool? And kind of—I don't know. Like Madame Tessier. She looks like she never got all frazzled up over someone in her life!"

"Do you think so?" Alex said dreamily. "I feel she . . . Her eyes are very expressive."

"You think, like with men she's really this terribly passionate person?"

He laughed. "I don't know. And I'm afraid I'm not going to have a chance to find out."

"Why don't you just, you know, ask her?"

"I should, I guess . . . I'm afraid she might be horrified."

"Why horrified?"

"Well, she thinks of me as this supposedly sensitive soul and here I want to drag her off to bed."

"Well, she knows you're human," Laura said.

"You don't think she'd mind?"

"I don't see why . . . I'd think she'd be flattered."

"The thing is, maybe she likes being admired from afar, but when it comes to actually—"

"Oh, I'm not saying she'll *do* anything," Laura said hastily, "but she might be pleased to know you wanted to."

Alex looked gloomy. "You don't think she'll want to?"

Laura laughed. "I don't know, Alex! I mean, wouldn't it be tricky? She *is* married, after all."

"Yeah, but they say French women always have all these affairs and lovers and stuff."

"She might be different."

"It's weird," Alex said. "On the one hand I want her to be different, I like that . . . But I don't want her to be *so* different she won't be interested."

"You have a problem on your hands," she said, looking at him with amusement.

"Listen, you know, it was great talking to you," he said. "I'm really glad we did. It's good to get a woman's point of view."

"I'm glad we talked too," she said shyly. "I hope she likes your song."

"I think you should just, you know, go out with people, maybe not *sleep* with them necessarily," he advised, "but maybe not be such a recluse."

"That's a good idea," she said.

"Like, if you ever want to just go to the movies or something, *I'd* be glad to go with you."

"Would you really?" she said. "That would be nice."

"Sure," he said. "I'd *like* to . . . I mean, even if I *do* have an affair with her, she'll still be busy *most* of the time."

Laura smiled. "True . . . Anyhow, good luck!"

He smiled back. "Thanks."

Later in the day Laura decided to walk home past the Quai de l'Horloge. She liked the brick and stone houses on the Place Dauphine. On one side she could see the Seine, dark, almost black in the evening light. She felt as though she had spent her whole time in Paris collecting places for herself and

David. It was as though he was inside her head. She talked to him inside her head, trying to share everything with him. When she wrote him and tried to explain, it didn't sound right. She never felt she captured what she felt. She had tried to tell him about Saint-Chapelle, the stained-glass windows. But the feeling it had aroused in her was something evanescent, something to do with the light at that moment, something to do with her loneliness which, somehow, lent all these places a magical intensity. I'll remember this forever, she kept thinking, forever. Someday we'll come back together, we'll walk down this street, we'll see everything that I'm seeing now, and it will be even more special.

7

There was a Christmas tree standing in the corner of the room. Alex sat at the piano, singing the song he had written.

"I'm really more of a writer than a singer," he said, "but here goes."

Madame Tessier looked disconcerted. He tried not to look at her. If only he had a decent voice! At one point he glanced at her and smiled, but she continued looking at him with her sphinxlike look. He finished his song with an amusing flourish. There was a long silence.

"Why did you sing me this song?" she said coolly.

He cleared his throat. "Well, you know the nine-teenth-century literature essay we were supposed to do? The comparison between classicism and romanticism?"

"Yes."

"Well, my song's kind of a romantic look at a classic situation."

"You wrote a song instead of the essay?"

He looked disappointed. "I guess you didn't like it, huh?"

She got up and walked to the window. "You still don't understand the French imperfect tense," she said crisply. "Your metaphors are feeble and your syntax primitive."

He felt devastated, but said softly, "I wasn't as concerned with the style as the content."

For a long minute she gazed at him. Then, turning, she said, "Why have you been following me?"

Alex turned red. "I—uh—don't know."

"At the beginning of the year I had high hopes for you," she said. "I'm disappointed, Alex. Your song was ridiculous, and you're being very foolish."

Desperation made him bold. "By being in love with you?"

"Yes."

"What's so foolish about that?"

"I am twice your age. I am thirty-five."

"I'm twenty," he said quickly.

"I could be your mother."

"So what?"

"You have invented me as a character in a romantic drama. You know *nothing* about me as I really am! It is all childish nonsense."

"I *do* know about you," he said. "I know you're beautiful and sensitive and that your husband is a clod and that you're unhappily married."

Her cheeks flushed. "How can you say such a thing? What do you know about my marriage? My husband is a very fine, a very—"

"He's a bastard," Alex said, angrily. "And *you* don't like him any more than I do."

"He is under many pressures due to his job," she began.

Alex was emboldened at having the upper hand. She had completely lost her cool. "Bullshit! So he has a job? Does that give him permission to torment students? Every time he says jump, you jump! Great! If that's what you want in a relationship, terrific."

She was staring at him in horror. "I don't think you have the right to say these things to me," she said.

"Yes, I do," he said. "Because they're true and you know it. . . . Listen, I'm not saying you should be in love with me or with anyone. I'm just saying you deserve something better out of life than a fathead like him. And if you have a lover or something, great! You should!"

She opened her mouth as though to speak and then stopped. "I'm afraid I can't talk about this anymore," she said. "You'll have to excuse me." She rushed out of the room, looking as though she was going to burst into tears.

Oh, shit! Alex sat there, depressed. What a dumb thing to do! You want to seduce her so you tell her her husband's a bastard, you get her all upset. Damn! He felt like going out and shooting himself.

Why couldn't I keep my stupid mouth shut? he thought.

That night he joined Joel and Toni at a bar. While Alex and Joel sat talking, Toni played pinball. Muttering in French, she pounded on the machine. Alex glanced at Joel. He was staring at Toni with a totally besotted expression on his face. Jesus, he has it bad, Alex thought. I hope she doesn't dump him or, if she does, she does it gently. He saw some French boys watching her as she moved at the machine, swaying her hips provocatively.

"It's funny," Alex said, "how at the beginning of the year I thought I was rooming with a real gnome."

"You were," Joel said.

"You know what you've done? You know what Toni means?"

"She means I almost flunked my midterms," Joel said. "Shit, I don't care anymore!"

"You scored a French girl," Alex said. "Those guys back there are saying, 'Why not me? Why Joel?' Which is a good question. What *does* she see in you?"

"Brute sex," Joel said, smiling wryly.

Alex sighed. "I have to remember not to hate you, but if I don't, remind me every once in a while."

"I'm sorry about what happened this afternoon," Joel said sympathetically.

"Oh, it was stupid," Alex said. "The whole thing, the song, everything I said. I messed up, but good. She'll probably never want to speak to me again."

"Still," Joel said. "She wouldn't have gotten so upset if what you said didn't hit home in some way."

"Yeah, but I should have done it differently! I practically made her cry!"

Later the three of them got up to leave. They walked down the dark, cold street together. Joel and Toni had their arms around each other. Alex walked with his hands behind his back, whistling tunelessly. Suddenly headlights flared and the familiar Stingray headed in their direction.

"That's her car!" Alex gasped. "Come on, let's go in here a minute."

He pushed them into a dark doorway. He waited, breathlessly. The car was approaching. He turned and looked at Toni and Joel. They were pressed up against the wall, kissing intently. Jesus, they'll be fucking in one minute, Alex thought. Damn! The car slowed to a stop.

"Alex, is that you?" Madame Tessier called out.

Alex's heart started beating a mile a minute. He stepped out of the doorway.

"Are you going home?" she asked.

He nodded, words having totally deserted him.

"Would you like a ride?"

He nodded again.

"Why don't you get into the car?"

"Uh—right." He went around to the other side, opened the door, and got in. They rode in silence. Alex glanced at her. She looked as though she'd been crying. About what? She glanced at him and smiled, but sadly.

"Are you—uh—okay?" he asked gently.

"Why?" she said quickly. "Do I look funny?"

"Well, you look like you've been crying," he said. "I hope what I said this afternoon didn't upset you or anything. Listen, it was really stupid."

"No, it wasn't that," she said.

"I mean, I didn't want to upset you," he rushed on. "I've felt terrible all afternoon, just thinking about it."

"It wasn't anything *you* did, Alex," she said. Her voice was soft and musical.

His heart flipped over, the way she'd used his name in that intimate voice.

"It's hard for me to talk about," she said. "Here, let me pull the car over a minute and I—" She drove off the road. It was very quiet. "You see," she said, not looking at him. "It seems Albert has been having an affair. I didn't know. I just found out a few days ago. I heard him arranging to meet her on the phone, and I—" She stopped, evidently unable to go on.

The bastard! Alex thought. The stupid bastard! "It just seems so—" he said, unable to express himself. "How can he be so *dumb?*"

She smiled, but tears were running down her cheeks. "That's so sweet of you to—"

Suddenly Alex leaned over and kissed her. He didn't even know he was going to. He just moved toward her and closed his eyes. Her mouth felt soft and moist. When it was over, he stared at her, breathless. "I—I'm sorry," he said.

"No, don't be."

"I'm in love with you," he said passionately. "I'm sorry. I can't help it."

She smiled. "It's nothing to be sorry about."

"I've been pestering you since I got here, following you around. I've been crazy. I'm not usually like this."

"Alex, it's so touching to me that you feel this way. I wish I deserved or merited such devotion."

"You do!" he said intensely.

She shook her head. "You don't know me. I have many faults, many flaws ... No doubt Albert found someone else because—"

"No!" Alex wouldn't let her finish. "He's just crazy, that's all."

"No," she insisted. "He says all the time I'm too absorbed in my work. That's true ... And perhaps I am not as, receptive to him as I once was. You see, I met him when I was seventeen. I thought he was God, I thought he knew everything. I had never had a lover before. He taught me everything, about love, about life . . . and now, well, I don't see him that way. He has shrunk—is that the right word?—to normal size. And perhaps he needs a woman with whom he can feel magically big and powerful again."

"Do you have a lover?" he said, hoping he didn't sound too stupid, but willing to risk anything.

She smiled. "No . . . Do I disappoint you? I know you want to think of me as the sophisticated Frenchwoman, worldly, knowledgeable."

"No, I just—"

"You wish you could be my lover?" she said, helping him.

He nodded.

"Well, maybe you can. Maybe that would be a good . . . solution for both of us."

Alex thought he was going to faint.

"He is going away to visit his . . . friend. Tomorrow. Maybe you can come and stay with me that night. What do you think?"

"Yes!" Alex said. "I want to!"

"I don't want to disillusion you ahead of time," she said, "but the fact is, you have probably had more sexual experience than I have."

"Two people?" he said wryly.

"That's one more than me," she said. "You don't mind? I would love to be the worldly older woman, but . . . Well, at least I'm older."

"You're wonderful!" he exclaimed. He couldn't believe this was happening! "I'm afraid you'll change your mind overnight."

"I won't," she said seriously. "I promise."

He swallowed. "Can I kiss you again?"

She nodded. "Yes."

He took her in his arms. This time it was a long, melting kiss. Her mouth opened; she let him put his tongue inside her mouth. He ran his hand down her smooth hair. He wanted her so much! If only she would do it in the car right now! Before she had a chance to change her mind. "I wish he had gone away already," he said, breathless.

"Yes." She smiled. "Well."

She had a dreamy far-off expression. Then suddenly she sighed. "I must go home at once," she said. She smiled. "I must help Albert to pack."

"Okay," Alex said magnanimously. "Help him pack."

"I will drive you home first."

*   *   *

At home, Alex lunged into the dark bedroom and grabbed Joel. "Hey! Wake up!"

"What?" Joel sat up sleepily and turned on the light. "What's going on? Are you crazy?"

"Yes!" Alex shouted. He felt alight with excitement. "He's going to Italy! Tomorrow!"

"Who? What the hell are you talking about?"

"Monsieur Tessier! Tomorrow morning."

"Yeah, and—"

"And she's picking me up tomorrow afternoon. And then she's taking me to her house. She wants me to spend the night with her!"

"Jesus!" Joel looked awake for the first time. "Where's our Scotch?" He got out of bed and found the bottle of Scotch.

"She loves me!" Alex said. "She wants me. I can't—I can't *believe* it." He told Joel about what had happened in the car.

"If it was anyone but you telling me this, I wouldn't believe you," Joel said.

"*I* don't believe it," Alex said. "Listen, it *happened* to me and I don't believe it . . . She's only slept with *one* person in her life—him. Can you imagine?"

107

"It's hard to."

"She said she was very shy. She went to some Catholic girls' school."

"Just like your fantasy about the island," Joel mused.

"What?"

"Your fantasy about the island and that girl. *She* was Catholic and shy."

"Yeah, hey, that's right," Alex said. "She's like that. She's like a fantasy."

Joel poured some Scotch for both of them. "You know, I feel a lot better now," he said. "I was beginning to feel really guilty about Toni and me."

"Now I don't have to hate you anymore," Alex said, gulping down the Scotch. "I don't have to lie there at night alone thinking of the two of you and going crazy."

Joel laughed. "I'm really glad, Alex."

Alex beamed. "Me too . . . I mean, I think I deserve it, don't you? I've been patient, I've been long-suffering—"

"You sure have."

"And the thing is, I really *do* love her. I'm not just feeding her a line. I'm in love with her! It's not like the thing with Susan. This is *real* love."

"It certainly sounds like it," Joel said.

"I mean, so she's thirty-five? So what? I'm mature for my age . . . And she looks much younger, don't you think? Twenty-five, maybe, at most. I mean, women marry men who are ten years younger nowadays. I saw a TV program on that."

"Listen, calm down . . . She's not going to *marry* you."

"Why not? Maybe she will. Look, he's a bastard, and—"

"Alex, just a sec . . . I hate to intrude with the cold light of reality, but, you *don't* have a profession, you *can't* support her, she's French . . . I mean, there are maybe nine million very good reasons why it could never happen."

"But we love each other!" Alex said. He had been drunk before he had any Scotch; now he felt like he was flying. "*That's* what counts! Who cares about that other stuff? I can get a job, I can support her—"

"In the style to which she's accustomed? Look at their place. Pretty swanky."

"She doesn't care about money!" Alex said heatedly. "She wants to be happy!"

"Look, you're going to have an affair with her. Great . . . Why push it beyond that?"

"I'm not! I just—" Suddenly he collapsed and fell on the bed. "But we'll be back home in half a year! I don't want to just sleep with her for half a year."

"Yesterday you would have cut off your right arm to sleep with her *once*," Joel reminded him.

"So? That was yesterday. Today is different. Yesterday I didn't know how she felt."

"Look, just take it easy, okay? I don't want to see you get hurt."

Alex looked at him. That was exactly what *he* had thought about Joel and Toni. "I can handle

myself," he said uncertainly. "Though I am a little
. . . I mean, what if I screw the whole thing up?
She's probably expecting some terrific lover. I don't
know."

"You'll be fine," Joel said encouragingly.

"He probably knows all these techniques, these
special things—"

"But you have your youthful impetuosity," Joel
said wryly.

"Yeah? Sure."

"Accept it. For some weird reason she likes you.
Why fight it?"

"Who's fighting it? I just want tomorrow to be
fantastic. I mean, it will be for *me,* but I want it to
be fantastic for *her.*"

"Look at me," Joel said. "I know nothing about
girls and women. Toni thinks I'm fantastic. Who
knows why?"

"Doesn't that make you nervous?"

"Sort of . . . But she says if a woman really is
turned on by a man, that she creates her own fantasy about him."

"Hmm." Alex pondered that. "What fantasy does
she have about me?"

"That you're madly in love with her. She's
flattered."

"But *millions* of men must be madly in love with
her."

"Only maybe millions aren't goofy enough to
trail her around for six months and write songs
about her."

Alex smiled. "So, my goofiness won the day? Well, who cares? God, I wish I believed in God."

"Why?"

"I'd pray that tomorrow would go well."

Joel finished his Scotch. "It will. Don't worry."

They turned off the light. Alex lay there, unable to sleep. I'll never be happier than I am now, he thought, no matter how long I live or what happens to me. Never. And he studied the room as though to memorize it, studied even Joel's sleeping face. And at some point, dazed by the intensity of his feelings, he fell sound asleep.

8

Toni was sitting next to Laura. Joel had brought her to the institute, partly to show her off, since Alex had suggested it. Laura was talking on intensely about some medieval festival she wanted to go to. "Since you're a native French person," she said, "I just thought you could tell these cultural meatballs how important the festival at Bourges is."

Toni smiled politely. "It sounds interesting, but I've never heard of it."

Laura looked amazed. "You haven't? Well, it's only the most famous medieval festival in the world! It occurs once every five years—and unless I can get a group together to go with me—"

"She's cute," Michael, one of the American students, said to Joel. "I wish *I* could meet someone like her."

Joel cleared his throat. "The problem is, you

hang around here too much. I picked Toni up at a local disco. She liked the way I danced."

Michèle, an institute staffer, came over to the table. "Toni?"

Toni turned around. She let out a little squeal. She and Michèle embraced like long-lost friends. "Where have you been?" Michèle said. "We haven't seen you in such a long time!"

"Oh, going to school, studying, my music."

"You two . . . know each other?" Joel said.

"Of course!" Michèle said. She turned. "Jean-Louis, *venez ici.* Look who's here!"

Jean-Louis came over and kissed Toni heartily on both cheeks. "Long time no see," he said. "How are you?"

"Well. And you?"

"*Ça va* . . . Nothing special."

"And what about Steven, Toni?" Michèle asked. "How's Steven?"

"I don't know," Toni said coolly.

Jean-Louis grinned. "You and Steven, the big romance."

Joel looked, horrified, at Toni. It had to be a total mistake!

Michèle smiled gaily. "Remember when the cleaning lady found Steven and you in the lounge the morning after the party? She almost had a heart attack."

The guys at the table began laughing. Joel felt as though a bulldozer had just swept over him, dividing him into two pieces. He looked down at his food, wanting nothing more than to disappear from the face of the earth permanently.

Another French girl wandered over. "Toni! What are you doing here?"

"Joel brought her," Melanie said. "*This* year."

The bitch! Joel glared at her. She smiled back at him innocently. He glanced at Laura. She was looking at him with concern. Toni wasn't looking at him at all.

"We heard Steven was accepted at the Harvard Law School," Christine said.

"I didn't know that," Toni said quietly. At least she was beginning to look somewhat uncomfortable, Joel noticed with satisfaction.

"Who's Steven?" Michael said. "Clue us in."

Michèle had disappeared for a minute. She returned with a big poster. It showed Toni, dressed in a short slip, evidently for some play, perched on a boy's knee. He was wearing shorts; his hand was between her legs. "*That's* Steven!" Michèle said cheerfully. "Cute, no?"

"Not my type," Michael said.

"It was from that silly play last year," Michèle went on blithely. "I wanted to hang it in my office, but Madame Tessier said it was not dignified."

Students from other tables were crowding around to see the poster.

"The institute ought to put *that* on the cover of its catalogue," Melanie said. "You'd get a lot more applications."

Joel looked desperately at Toni. She looked back at him with a very cool expression, as though he were some blind date she was trying to decide how to get rid of. Dying must be like this, he thought—something like it.

He didn't remember anything about the rest of the meal. He ate, but all he could think of was the poster and the way she had looked' sitting there with that expression he had thought—or wanted to think—was reserved just for him. So there was one every year! Since when? Since she was seventeen? Sixteen? He didn't want to think about it. Maybe this year she thought she'd try someone with dark hair, or a Jew, just for variety, just for change. Why not? What was there to lose? If he was a bad lover, she'd just slip out and find someone else. It was no big deal.

They walked down the street in silence. Joel felt too bitter and hurt to say anything.

"Well, you've certainly got terrific taste in men," he said finally.

"I *knew* you would be like this!" she exclaimed. "I *knew* it!"

"Like what?"

"Jealous! Petty jealousy! You were like that with Pascal."

"Look, they had a goddamn *billboard* with your photo on it!"

"So?"

"So, why didn't you take porno movies of you doing it with him and sell them around the block! Or *did* you and they didn't happen to have those along today?"

"You have a dirty mind," she said coldly.

"Sure, *I* have a dirty mind," he said. "You were just sitting there letting him feel you up because he reminded you of your aunt!"

"You're trying to make this into a big deal."

"*I'm* not making it into a big deal. *You* did, by not telling me!"

Toni stopped and turned to him. "Look, I haven't even *heard* from Steven since he left. He said he'd write me and he didn't We made a lot of plans but nothing happened. Okay?"

Joel felt even worse at the thought that she had been ditched. "So you thought you'd have better luck this year," he said bitterly.

"Yes!" she said. "I thought so, but evidently I was wrong! Evidently I didn't allow for the fragility of the male ego! . . . Look, I never pretended to be a virgin. If you thought so, you're just a fool. I *have* been around the block, you know!"

"Around the block! What's *that* supposed to mean?"

"It's a good American expression," she said.

"Well, nobody uses it," he said furiously.

"Raymond Chandler does!" She snorted. "Quit acting like an idiot."

"Look who's talking," Joel said, "our resident institute groupie."

Suddenly her cheeks blazed; she looked furious. "So, why were you showing me off like a hunting trophy?"

Joel's heart sank. "I—I didn't mean . . ."

"You *did* mean!" she rushed on. "You meant to say—'Look at me, fellas! Look what *I've* got!' And you didn't think for one *second* of how humiliated I would feel. Steven would *never* have done something like that."

"Well, you lost him. I guess once he got back to America he decided it wasn't worth it." He regretted this stupid cruelty almost as soon as the words left his mouth.

"Just like you, huh?" she said. "Your little French affair that you can talk about with your friends at home! Charming!"

"It wasn't like that," he said desperately.

"Yes, of course. It was true love. Sure! Tell that to the horse marines! And *quit* following me!"

Joel stopped dead in his tracks. "I'm not following you."

"Just go away!" she said furiously. "Or are you afraid, like you're afraid of everything, afraid of some guy from last year, of what your friends think? You're just a yellow-belly!" She turned and stormed off.

"What does that *mean?*" Joel called after her. "If you don't know English, don't use it!"

"Coward!" she yelled. "You're a *coward!*"

He stood there, stunned. It was all over. Jesus. "Now I don't have to envy you anymore," Alex had said, "imagining the two of you together." Oh no! He walked back toward their apartment. Right now Alex was probably in seventh heaven. I don't want to think about it! Shit!

Why, in God's name, had he taken Toni to the institute? Why had Alex made that dumb suggestion about showing her off? "Like a hunting trophy," she had said. She was sensitive. Of *course* she felt badly. "Steven wouldn't do that." Fuck Steven! Joel knew that if by pressing a button he could have eliminated Steven from the face of the earth he would have done so immediately with immense pleasure and satisfaction. But what good would *that* do? How would *that* help? For a bewildered moment, he buried his face in his hands. What am I going to *do?* You're going to go home and take a nap, a calmer part of himself advised. And when you wake up, you'll feel better.

Okay, he replied to this sane advice. That's exactly what I'm going to do.

* * *

Walking through the Tessier house, Alex kept remembering Joel's comment about: "Can you support her in the manner to which she is accustomed?" It was a very elegant home, which clearly had cost a lot of money.

"Do you like it?" she asked. "We decorated it in what we call Eisenhower Fifties Style. It's very hard to find good American nineteen-fifties furniture in Paris. It's amusing, isn't it?"

"Not when your parents live in it," Alex said. He sat down beside her on the hard, unyielding couch. Now what? Did you just do it? Did you lead up to it? It was afternoon, and all the magic of the night before seemed to have vanished. He reached out and took her in his arms. He tried to kiss her. She pulled back and glanced at her watch.

"I feel so nervous!" she said. "Albert's plane leaves at seven. Until then perhaps we should—cool it, as you say?"

"Oh, sure," Alex said, relieved in a way. He didn't even feel in the mood, now that the time had come. Maybe just nervousness. God, I pray it comes back later, he thought.

She took him into the den. There was a big map of Europe on the wall. Little red flags stuck out at various places. "Each flag will someday be a new institute," she said. "That is our plan. One in every major city."

He was standing right behind her. Impulsively he kissed her neck. She turned and he pretended to be studying the map. "Sort of like hamburger franchises," he said. "Uh—then what will you do?"

"Move to Los Angeles," she said coolly. She pulled one flag off the map. "This is where Albert will soon be with his . . . friend. The bastard." She broke the little flag in two.

"He doesn't matter," Alex said, wanting to comfort her.

"Well . . ." She looked sad.

"*I* love you," he said. "That's all that matters!"

She smiled at him. "Yes," she said, but more as though she were humoring him than as if she meant it.

He frowned. "Do we *have* to wait until seven o'clock?" he said, wanting her right away.

"Well, we should. I couldn't really enjoy it if I was worried."

He wanted her to enjoy it. "Okay."

"Meanwhile, we can go in our hot tub."

"Your what?"

"You have them in America, no? It is an American invention. Ours is new."

She showed him the hot tub, which was out on the patio. God, they must have money.

"I never saw one before," he admitted.

"Never?" She looked amazed.

"Only in magazines."

"But I thought in America everyone had one."

"Maybe rich people . . . Or people in California or something. Not college teachers in Pennsylvania."

"Oh?" She looked surprised. "You want to try it?"

He swallowed. "Sure, why not." He looked at her, wondering who was supposed to take their clothes off first. What if she didn't like his body? He stood there, frowning, then decided—what the hell!—took off his clothes, and climbed in gingerly. "Yow! It's hot!" he said.

"My husband likes it like this." She undressed carefully and slowly, draping her things over a chair, as though she were alone. He tried not to stare at her as she climbed in.

"You like it?" she said.

It was a strange feeling—the steaming water all around him. "Yeah, it's kind of—"

"It's supposed to be an erotic experience," she said gravely.

"Being with *you* is an erotic experience," he said,

kissing her. She was wet and gleaming, younger looking, even, with her hair wet at the ends.

"I don't look like a twenty-year-old," she said. "I know that. You don't have to lie."

"You look better," he said. "A *million* times better."

Being in the big tub was both erotic and not. The hot water made him feel sleepy, but sitting next to her, glimpsing her naked body through the water, woke him up. He reached out and touched her under the water. Holding her around the waist, he kissed her. He remembered movies where people had fucked underwater. How? Well, not for the first time. The logistics of it were too complicated.

"I think I want to get out," she said. "My hands are getting all—" She showed him her fingertips, which were wrinkly from the warm water. She slipped out and came back wrapped in a huge orange bath towel. "Come, don't you want to get warm and dry?" she said.

Alex got out of the tub and shook the water from his hair. He walked over to her. He was slightly embarrassed to have her see he was aroused, but then he thought: What does she expect, if we take a nude bath together? To his surprise she opened up the big towel and held it out in back of her like a cape. When he came close to her, she enveloped him in it, closing the two of them inside the towel. He stood there, his body pressed against hers.

"What time is it?" he said.

She laughed. "Slow down! All good things must be savored, you know?"

Yes! Christ, he had to remember that. He *had* to slow down, even if it killed him, which it probably would. They walked together into the bedroom and lay down together, still with the towel wrapped around them. He let his hand wander all over her body. "You're so incredibly beautiful," he said in wonderment. "I can't believe it."

"Not too thin?" she said anxiously.

"No." He couldn't believe she would have any self-doubts about her body. "Not too anything. Perfect."

"I used to be too thin," she said. "But now—"

"I saw you naked once," he said. "Months ago."

"What?" She stared at him. "You're joking!"

"No." He told her about the jeans store and watching her.

"Alex!" She laughed. "You are too much!"

"Oh, God," he said. "It was horrible!"

"Horrible?"

"Seeing you and not being able to do anything about it, watching you do that little dance."

She blushed. "I like to dance . . . I'm not very good."

"Yes, you are," he said passionately. "You're good at everything."

"No." She had that half-sad smile. "Alex, really, don't idealize me so much. You'll be disappointed."

"I'm not," he said. "You're perfect, I'm not idealizing you."

"I'm shy," she said. "I feel awkward, even now, being here with you, even having decided to do it."

"You do?" He loved her even more for feeling

awkward. "You're so beautiful! Any man in the world would want you. How can you not know that?"

"You see me that way," she said. "You are—how do they say?—blinded by love."

"Yes," he said, kissing her. "I am. . . . But you're also perfect." He wanted her so much he thought he might die. Please, don't go too fast, he begged himself.

He kissed her breasts and belly and thighs all over; her skin was so soft! When he tried to kiss her between her legs, she pulled slightly on his hair. He looked up at her. "You don't have to do that," she said softly.

"I want to," he said.

She was frowning. "Are you sure? Albert never . . . liked it."

"Albert is a total shithead," he said.

"Only do it if you really want to," she said pleadingly.

"I'll only do it if you want me to . . . Do you?"

She looked hesitant. "Yes," she said finally.

She was so clean and fragrant, everywhere. After she had come, she drew him up and kissed him passionately. "I love you," she said. "Thank you . . . Let me do it for you. Do you want me to?"

"I—" But before he could say anything she had taken him in her mouth and was making love to him that way. He lay there with his eyes closed, feeling strange, almost as though he weren't there, as though he were floating around the room. It reminded him of once when he'd smoked some pot that was much stronger than he'd expected.

"It's past seven," he said when she had stopped and was just lying there, hugging him around the waist, her cheek pressed to his stomach.

"Okay," she said softly. "I have to go inside just for a moment. You'll wait for me?"

He smiled. As though he would do anything else! "I'll wait for you," he said.

* * *

Joel walked slowly down the street, toward the institute. He felt better, a million times better. His saner self had been right. He had had a long heavy nap, falling into sleep as though into a drug. When he woke up, he washed his face with cold water and went out to eat. He went to a good restaurant, not just a student hangout, and he had a good meal— *boeuf bourguignon*, a glass of red wine, a salad, a pear tart with strong coffee for dessert. He remembered once talking about food with Laura, who claimed she had a weight problem and loved to eat. "I mean, the trouble is," she'd said, "there are so many different *kinds* of good food—fruit and ice cream and lamb chops and pizza. If I'm feeling good, I want to eat to celebrate, and if I'm feeling bad I want to eat to console myself. It's lousy!"

Out on the street again, Joel felt consoled. He felt sad, but not totally devastated as he had a few hours earlier. I'm in terrible pain, he admitted, but I can survive. It will take a while, but I can do it.

He felt as though he'd fallen from a very steep cliff and was feeling himself all over for broken bones. Occasionally, inadvertently, a memory of Toni would flash through his mind, her body, her face in bed, and he would wait, almost patiently, as though he were being tortured by the enemy. There's nothing worse than this, he told himself. If you can get through moments like that, you'll make it.

As he passed by the institute, Christine and Monsieur Tessier came out. Monsieur Tessier! Joel stopped dead in his tracks. Alex! My God! Monsieur Tessier was walking toward his car. Joel grabbed Christine by the arm. "Monsieur Tessier's back?" he said. "Why? What happened?"

"There was a strike at the airport," Christine said.

"Is he . . . going home?" Joel said. "Does Madame Tessier know?"

"No—when he heard she was ill, he didn't want to call in case she was resting in bed. Why?"

"In bed," Joel said. "Oh my God." He saw Monsieur Tessier getting into his car and starting the engine, Joel started running. The car was pulling away from the curb. He leapt in front of it. Monsieur Tessier put on the brakes. Out of breath, Joel walked around to the side window, trying desperately to think of something to say. Finally he blurted out, "Would you like to get a beer or something?"

"Beer? What are you talking about?" Tessier's cold, contemptuous expression made it clear he thought Joel was out of his mind.

"I just thought . . . well, maybe we could talk," Joel said. "I have this problem, and I—well, I thought I should tell you about it."

"You have a problem?" Monsieur Tessier said. "What problem?"

Joel swallowed. "It's kind of personal," he said. "And sort of complicated. Do you think we could take about it? It wouldn't take too long."

"How long?"

"Oh, just maybe half an hour," Joel said.

Monsieur Tessier hesitated. "All right," he said, turning the motor off again.

On the way to the *bar-tabac*, Joel began trying to think of what his problem could be. Ad-lib it, anything! he said. You have a good imagination. If only he could get to a phone and warn Alex! Jesus!

"I've been feeling very . . . suicidal," he said over the beer. "I've been seriously considering taking my own life . . . but I thought that might not be polite to you and Madame Tessier."

"Polite?"

"Well, I know you try and make us happy, and the thing is, it's not your school. It's—I just—I fell in love with someone."

Monsieur Tessier smiled for the first time. "Ah? So? A French girl?"

Joel nodded.

"She is very lovely?" Monsieur Tessier said, seeming to warm to the subject. "Very charming?"

Joel sighed. "Yes, very . . . Only today I discovered that . . . that I wasn't the first."

Monsieur Tessier tried to look grave. "You had thought you were?"

Joel swallowed. "Well, I guess I knew, but I—"

He smiled. His face looked more compassionate than Joel had ever seen it look. "Love is a difficult thing," he said. "I remember my first love. I fell in love with an older woman, the classic *affaire*, you know? She was not so old really, twenty-seven, but I was sixteen. Oh, how beautiful she seemed to me! She worked at a store near my parents' home, a pastry store, and I would save up my money every day to go in to buy one *croissant*, one roll."

"Then what happened?" Joel said, interested, almost forgetting about Alex.

"She agreed to meet me. We went away for one weekend, one wonderful, magnificent weekend which I will never, *ever* forget . . . And then she went back to her husband. I was—how do you say?—devastated. Like you, I wanted to die. I thought of all the methods. I wanted to choose the one which would make her feel most terrible. Poison? Throwing myself before a train? But you know how it is." He smiled. "We are all cowards, luckily. We wake up one morning and the sun is shining and we see a pretty girl and soon, gradually, we heal. . . . You will heal," he told Joel. "I promise you."

Joel stared at him. He had never expected to *like* Monsieur Tessier. "She's just different from American girls," he said. "She's—"

"Of course. French girls are very . . . feminine? What do you say? They enjoy being women. Unlike

American women, the ones I have met. They glory in their femininity."

Joel began feeling depressed again. "Yes," he said.

"She still loves you," Monsieur Tessier said. "You have just had a little fight. You must be magnanimous. Show her you forgive her. So she has had others? Forgive!"

Joel frowned. "You would forgive?" he said.

"Of course!"

"You think she really loves me? I was awful to her. I said cruel things."

"We all say cruel things to people we love."

"I feel like my heart is broken," Joel said.

Monsieur Tessier patted his hand and smiled gently. "You are a true romantic," he said. "I fear your heart is very tender, no?"

Joel smiled sheepishly. "I'm afraid so."

"You will recover," Monsieur Tessier said. "You will survive and prosper."

Suddenly Joel remembered why they were there. "The thing is, when I was feeling depressed before, I took all these pills—downers, uppers, stuff you probably never heard of. Do you think I should go to the hospital?"

"Perhaps . . . Let me see. Come with me, first. I must drop my things off at home and let Martine know I am back. Then I will take you to the hospital."

"But—why don't you just call her?" Joel said. "Let her know you're back?"

"Why call when we are five minutes away? You are done? Good!"

Unable to think of any further excuse, Joel followed him in dread.

* * *

Alex lay in bed, waiting. Two small bed lights were on, casting a warm glow around the room. It's finally going to happen, he thought. He felt both excited and calm. Finally Madame Tessier came out of the bathroom. She was wearing a robe. Slowly she let it drop to the floor. She stood there one moment, looking at him. She looked like a statue, a vision, unreal. It seemed to Alex the whole room was starting to glow. Then, in horror, he realized it was the glare of headlights from a car coming up the drive. He looked at the window quickly and back at Madame Tessier. "Who's that?"

She frowned. "I don't know." She moved to the window. "My God, my husband!"

"Oh shit!" Alex said.

"Well, maybe this is good," she said nervously, putting on her robe. "We have nothing to hide."

Alex whipped out of bed and began getting dressed as fast as he could. "Nothing to hide? What about *me?*" Pulling on his shirt, he rushed down the hall. "Where's the back door?"

"Alex, don't leave," said Madame Tessier. "It's more honest this way."

"Sure, honesty's fun, but what about the exhilaration of deceit—and escape?" He reached the end of the hall and found the back door. He turned and kissed her gently. "I'll figure out a way we can see each other again," he said, in a low, tender voice. "Believe me, nothing's going to keep us apart now—" He opened the door and found himself face to face with Monsieur Tessier and Joel. "Except death, maybe."

Joel and Monsieur Tessier advanced into the living room. Alex and Madame Tessier retreated.

"Albert, what are you doing here?" Madame Tessier said nervously, pulling her robe tightly around her.

"He didn't go to Italy," Joel said—"There was a plane strike."

"What are *you* doing here?" Alex said to Joel.

"He took an overdose of drugs," said Monsieur Tessier. "What are *you* doing here?"

"I—uh—" Alex began.

"We were about to make love!" Madame Tessier said boldly.

"Well, sounds like it's been a big night for everybody," Joel said cheerfully, nervously. "Maybe we should get going, huh, Alex?"

"I'll kill him," Monsieur Tessier said in a quiet voice. He lunged at Alex. Madame Tessier and Joel grabbed him, holding his arms.

"Stop it, Albert!" Madame Tessier said. "It's your fault!"

"My fault! Let go of me!" He knocked away his wife's restraining hand and suddenly got Joel in a headlock.

"You've got the wrong guy," Joel said, choking.

Alex grabbed a candlestick and approached them.

"Running away with Yvette!" Madame Tessier cried. "The girl at the answering service! How pitiful!"

Monsieur Tessier shoved Joel out of the way. Joel fell coughing into a chair. Alex lowered the candlestick.

"I didn't run away," Monsieur Tessier said. "I didn't go to Italy."

Her cheeks were blazing. She had clearly forgotten Alex existed. "You've gone other places with Yvette! I looked into it—I know all about your affair with her!"

"And what's *this*?" Monsieur Tessier said, glaring at Alex. "What about *him*? You find some boy from the school to take to bed with you. For what—revenge?"

Alex watched them, horrified. He couldn't believe what was happening; he didn't want to.

"*You* were never above picking up students," Madame Tessier cried. "Were you, Albert? What about me, when I was your student?"

"At the university?" he said. "All you were interested in was a good grade from your professor. Well, you got it, didn't you? And you also got your professor—to run your ridiculous school for morons like *them!*" He gestured wildly at Joel and Alex, who stood dumbfounded, watching them.

Joel handed Alex his coat. "Come on."

After a moment Alex followed him.

They walked through the neon sleaziness of Pigalle. Striptease, seedy bars, sordid hotels. Heavily made-up faces loomed out of doorways; taunting hookers tailed them.

They stopped for a drink at a bar.

"I always thought Montmartre would be more . . . artistic," Joel said. "Toulouse-Lautrec and all that."

"Maybe it was, once," Alex said. But in the dark bar the atmosphere was like a bar anywhere—the tackiness didn't seem especially French or especially romantic. Even the words emblazoned outside, *Strip Tease*, took their cue from Forty-second Street. Trying to imitate the worst of American culture. It was weird. Not like the small café where he went to hear jazz sometimes, which had a certain ambience, with its small round tables and faded wallpaper.

"Well, listen, *my* day wasn't so terrific either," Joel said.

"What're you talking about?" Alex said gloomily.

Joel told him.

"So?" Alex said.

Joel felt angry. "What do you mean—so?"

"So, she's slept with other guys! Big deal!" He sounded bitter.

Joel was taken aback. "She picks one up every year, evidently. It's an institute tradition!"

"So what? So you're the one for this year? What are you bitching about?"

"I thought she was in love with me."

"Maybe she is. She falls in love easily, evidently."

"And out."

"And out . . . So, what did you expect? She'd take a vow of chastity?"

Joel sighed. "Yeah, I guess—"

"Listen, I'm sorry, I'm just not in a very sympathetic mood tonight . . . God, I don't know. I feel like killing myself."

Joel laughed.

"What's so funny?"

He told him about the conversation with Monsieur Tessier.

"Maybe we should do it together," Alex said, smiling wryly.

Joel smiled back. "He's right. We'll survive. We'll wake up one morning and the sun will be shining and—"

"Joel, you don't *know*," Alex said intensely. "She was so *beautiful!*"

"Nothing happened?" Joel said.

"Oh, no, it's just—we never actually *did* it. She kept saying wait till it's safe, wait till he's on the plane." Alex pounded his fist. "Why did there have to be a fucking plane strike! Shit!"

"Well," Joel said helplessly.

"Damn the French! They can't run *anything* efficiently. What a country!"

Joel sighed. "Laura said that's their charm. They care about form, not content."

Alex looked disgusted. "The hell with all of them!"

"She said it's just another approach to life. They care about beauty, about art . . ."

"Sure," Alex said. "They have no *feelings*, that's all! It's all form, right? . . . no content. Love is just . . . some kind of ballet for them. You do the right steps, you change partners, it's all . . . meaningless."

"It's just—" Joel said stumblingly. "Toni was . . . different from American girls."

Alex smiled at him sadly. "I know! Madame Tessier was too."

"She was so . . . she seemed to love making love. She didn't seem to have any hangups, any—"

"Fuck!" Alex said. "We sure screwed up . . . Well, one thing I *know*. I'm not going back to the institute. Madame Tessier can have her predigested culture."

"What're you going to do?"

"You realize this year is our last chance. Coming to Paris is our last great escape. What's waiting at home for you?"

"I don't know."

"Reality," Alex said. "Like, what're you going to do when you finish college next year?"

"Well," Joel said, "I thought I might try to get a job on—"

"Worse, what're you going to do after that with your life?"

"I had it all planned," Joel said. "Now I'm not so sure."

Alex looked cheerful again. "So, what do you say we just take off?"

Joel stood up. "Yeah, I got a class in a couple of hours. I'll get the check."

Alex put his hand on his shoulder. "Sit down. I meant, let's get out of here and see things. Go to Greece! Italy!"

Joel sat down. He looked at him, puzzled. "Actually take off?"

"Yeah, actually take off! Do exactly what we want, pick up girls, have a ball."

"But what about our studies?"

"What about it? Who gives a shit! It's all garbage."

Joel looked uncertain. "I don't know."

"Oh, you never know anything!" Alex said disgustedly. "Take a chance for once in your life! Do something! Live!"

"Let me sleep on it, okay? . . . Not that there's much of the night left. But I mean metaphorically."

"You and your metaphors! God! Okay, let's go home. If we're not going to kill ourselves, we might as well at least get a good night's sleep."

"True."

They strolled slowly toward the door.

In bed, in the dark, Joel said, "Well, so much for the idea of going after French women. . . . We come four thousand miles to get dumped on."

"Those are the breaks," Alex said. He sounded sleepy.

9

"You're really going?" Laura said. She had run into Joel outside the institute. He was loaded down with suitcases, bags of food.

"Yeah, Alex has it all planned—Barcelona, Valencia—"

She looked envious. "I'd go, only—well, I'd hate to lose credit for this whole year."

Joel looked worried. "I know . . . I worry about that. Alex doesn't seem to care."

"How come?"

Joel hesitated. He told Laura a little about what had happened with Madame Tessier. "I guess he's kind of fed up with everything," he concluded.

"The poor thing," Laura said sympathetically. "She really ditched him, huh?"

"Well, it was the plane strike basically," Joel

said. "If it wasn't for that, they would have had a red-hot affair."

"Oh, bullshit!" Laura said vehemently. "If she really loved him, she'd have found a way to see him anyway. So her husband came back? So what?"

Joel's eyes widened. "That's—an interesting way of looking at it."

"She's just fooling around with him," Laura said contemptuously. "He's a sucker to fall for it."

Joel began feeling very depressed, thinking of Toni. "I guess he was in love with her," he said, "and when you're in love—"

"What?" Laura demanded belligerently. "You lose your head totally? Not *me!* I *never* would!"

"Not even about David?"

"David's a nice *person*," she insisted. "We really *love* each other . . . Hey, what happened with Toni, by the way? Did you make up?"

He shook his head.

"How come?"

"Well . . . I don't know."

"Joel! Hey, come on! You can't let it just go like that. Call her up! Say you're sorry."

"For what?"

She looked incredulous. "For *what?* Boy, boys are really something. For *acting* that way! Say you didn't mind about that poster, that you realize it was all in fun."

"But I *do* mind," he said. "I mind a lot."

"Why?"

"Why?" He was surprised she couldn't understand. "Because she—it shows she just picks people up like—hot potatoes and then drops them."

"It does *not* show that," Laura said.

"What *does* it show, then?"

"It shows she's had other guys . . . So what? You would've had other girls if you weren't so shy. It's no credit to you. It's not like you're more moral or something. You were just scared!"

Joel swallowed. "Well, still . . ."

"Still what? You mean you're going off on this trip without even seeing her? God, that takes the cake! I thought you were in love, supposedly!"

"I was, I am," he stammered.

"Don't you even care how she feels?"

"I—"

"Listen, she probably feels awful right this *second*. Absolutely *awful*. How can you be so cruel? I mean it, Joel. I'm absolutely shocked that you would do that."

Joel stood there, stunned. "But I don't think she wants to see me again. She said I was a coward."

"You are! Of course she wants to see you again!"

"How do you know?"

"Because she's in love with you, you dodo! Anyone could tell that."

"They could?"

"Sure! The way she looked at you and everything . . . She's probably home crying her eyes out right this second."

Joel sighed. "Or in bed with someone she picked up last night."

"Joel Weber!" Laura said severely. "I don't like

to be mean, but I will. You don't deserve her! You know that? That was a nasty, awful thing to say! And it would serve you right if she never spoke to you again."

"Laura, listen," Joel protested. "You've got it all wrong. I'd do anything to get her back."

"So *do* something!"

"What?"

Laura looked exasperated. "Joel, you're not dumb! Think of something. Pretend you're her. Get her some terrific present, a bunch of flowers or a basket of peaches or something."

"Peaches?"

"If she likes them . . . Or a book of poetry. *You* know. Something to show you still love her."

"But I'm going away."

"Listen, I have to go," Laura said. "*You* figure it out, okay?"

"Okay."

On the way to the train station Joel kept thinking of the conversation with Laura. It was interesting how totally different it was talking to a girl, what a different point of view she had. Was she right? *Was* Toni crying her eyes out? *Had* he been unfair?

In the train compartment he sat reading aloud from the guidebook while Alex shoved their bags onto the rack. "After Toulouse, we cross the border into Andorra. Then we—"

"Great!" Alex exclaimed. "That's the route Hannibal took over the Pyrenees when he invaded Gaul."

"After Barcelona we can follow the Mediterranean south to Valencia."

"Valencia! The golden towers where El Cid beat the Moors!"

"And then," Joel looked up. "Granada and the Alhambra, the most romantic monument in Spain." He closed the book, handed it to Alex, and reached for his suitcase.

"What're you doing?" Alex said in amazement.

"I'm not going."

"Goddamn it, I knew it! I *knew* you'd do this."

"Well, you were right," Joel said sheepishly.

"You chickenshit!" Alex shouted, oblivious of the other people in the compartment. "I thought you'd changed. What's wrong?"

"What am I going to tell my parents?"

"Your parents! Oh, Christ, Joel!"

Joel started down the aisle; Alex followed him.

"I can't just drop out halfway through," Joel said. "I'll lose the whole year. They might not even accept me back at Columbia!"

"I'm not talking about school," Alex said intensely. "I'm talking about *life!*"

"Alex, you're not," Joel said patiently. "You're dreaming. This is just another fantasy, like Madame Tessier—"

Alex looked hurt. "Okay, go back to the institute, finish college, find a good job—so maybe in ten years you can afford to come back here and go to Spain! Why not go now?"

The train lurched forward. Joel clambered down

to the last step. He turned and looked at Alex. "I can't," he said quietly. He jumped down.

Alex leaned out and looked back at Joel on the platform as the train pulled out. "Why not?" he shouted.

"I don't know," Joel shouted back. "Have a good trip! Write me, okay?"

Alex nodded and waved. Joel stood watching the train pull out from under the vaulted station into the daylight beyond. Feeling rotten, he picked up his suitcase and walked away.

*   *   *

Joel stood staring into the store window a long time. Finally he walked in. He looked surreptitiously around for Toni, but couldn't see her. At the front was one of the other girls, one of her friends. "Uh—is Toni here?" he asked.

The girl—Malsy, her name was, he remembered—looked embarrassed. "She left."

He frowned. "When will she be back?"

"She's not coming back."

Joel swallowed. His heart began thumping painfully. "What do you mean? Where'd she go?"

"She wouldn't tell us. She said something about going to Marseilles . . . Her parents left too. They *all* went away."

Joel felt suspicious. "This doesn't make any sense," he said. "She didn't even leave an address?"

"That's all I know, Joel," Malsy said, looking

142

sympathetic. "I'm sorry." She began ringing up a customer's bill.

He stood there, staring at her, confused. It was obviously just a story. Toni didn't want to see him. She'd told her friends to make up some idiotic thing to tell him. He felt awful. Well, so much for that, Laura, and your terrific theories about how madly in love with me she is.

He walked slowly down the street. Suddenly he heard his name.

"Joel."

He turned. It was Toni. She ran until she caught up with him.

"Where did you come from?" he said.

She hesitated. "I was hiding in the back of the store."

He looked puzzled. "Why?"

"I didn't think I wanted to see you again."

"Oh . . . Well, what made you change your mind?"

She shrugged.

They walked along side by side. Joel felt as though he were being slowly sawed in two. She looked so lovely!

"Your friends said you were going to Spain," Toni said.

"Alex went."

"You didn't want to go."

"No, I wanted to."

"Why didn't you?"

"I—I don't know. I didn't want to miss the year,

lose all that credit." He forced himself to look at her. "You."

"Me?"

"I—didn't want to leave like that, after we'd had that fight . . . Listen, Toni, I'm sorry, I said some stupid, cruel things. I didn't mean them."

"Didn't you?" she said coolly.

"I was hurt," he said. "I—I wanted, I guess, to think I was special for you the way you were for me."

After a moment she said quietly, "You *are* special."

He glanced at her, pierced through by the way she had said that.

"So I've had other boyfriends?" she said. "So what? If you had had other girls, you'd realize it isn't such a big thing. Not everyone finds what they are looking for the first time out."

"Laura said something like that."

"Your American girl friend?"

"She's not my girl friend . . . just a friend."

"She seemed nice . . . She didn't want to console you by getting you into bed?"

Joel had to smile at the thought. "Laura? Are you kidding? She's in love with this guy David, back in the States. Anyway, even if she wasn't, she'd never be interested in *me*."

"How do you know?"

"I just *know!* She thinks I'm—well, weird, sort of. She doesn't think of me that way at *all*."

Toni smiled. "You're so naïve, Joel."

"I am?"

"Of *course* she likes you. I could tell by the way she looked at you."

"No!" Joel said. "Absolutely not. I mean, it's very flattering that you think so, but she wouldn't go to bed with me if I was the last person in Paris."

"And would you with her?"

He was startled. "Me with Laura?"

"Yes. What if she had, shall we say, offered herself to you after our fight? What then?"

He couldn't imagine it. "I can't imagine it."

"Try."

"Well, I— She's very pretty, but—"

"You would have turned her down flat?" There was a mischievous smile on her face.

He smiled. "Well, maybe if she had insisted, wouldn't take no for an answer—"

"See!" Toni cried triumphantly. "You're no different! You're just like everyone else."

Joel laughed. "You may have something there." He stopped. "Come here just one second. I want to see something."

She stopped. He took her in his arms and kissed her. It was a long, passionate kiss. When it was over, she smiled at him. "So? Did you find out what you wanted to know?"

"Yes," he said. He took her hand. She still loved him! Laura was right.

Back at her place, they undressed hurriedly and got into bed with almost grim faces, as though they were going to an operation which had to be performed to save a dying person. He entered her right away and she seemed ready, as though all the days in between had been leading up to this. "I love you," he said as he came. "I love you so much!" Afterward she looked up at him with that sleepy tender look. "I love you too," she said softly, "even if you're crazy."

They lay contentedly with their arms around each other. "The last few days were . . . hell," Joel said. "I hope I never go through anything like that again."

"They were bad for me too . . . But I felt so mad at you I couldn't see straight. And we had a concert to perform. I had to concentrate on that. Alphonse told me to forget all about you. He said American men were no good."

"Who's Alphonse?" Joel asked, jealous.

"Our harpsichordist."

"Is he interested in you?"

"Well, he's married to Françoise, our cellist. He likes me . . ."

"You didn't feel like picking someone up just to get even with me?"

"I thought of it, but I decided it would be childish. I knew it was just what you'd expect me to do. I decided to confound your expectations."

He smiled. "Clever."

"I am very clever," she said. "Anyway, you make too much of sex."

"I do?"

"Yes . . . So, if I had slept with someone? I didn't, but if I had? So what?"

"Well." Even the thought of it gave him terrible pain. "I don't know."

"So, if you had slept with Laura? What then? You would have enjoyed it, she too . . . It wouldn't have had anything to do with us."

"No." He could see that. "I'm not in love with her."

"It would have been—how do you say?—good, clean fun."

Joel laughed. "Poor Alex," he said after a moment.

"Why?"

He told her about the debacle with Madame Tessier.

"He gave up too easily," Toni said. "He should have come back the next day."

"But she didn't seem to give a damn about him."

"That was in front of her husband! What does he expect?"

"Well, his feelings were hurt."

Toni looked pensive. "I feel sorry for her."

"For Madame Tessier?"

"Yes . . . She must love Alex."

"She must?"

"Yes . . . She has . . . fallen for him. And now he deserts her. What is it about American men? You have no—staying power."

Joel frowned. "But she—I don't know."

Toni sighed. "It is very sad. She is missing him very much right now, I know!"

Joel wished Alex could be there to hear that. "You really think so?"

"Oh yes, I know it! Here he left her all—aflame. What can she do?"

"Sleep with her husband?"

"Him! You saw him. A cold fish."

"Gosh, I wish Alex had thought of this. . . . He just thought she had dumped him. He and I were going to kill ourselves together. A joint suicide. Done in by the cold hearts of French women!"

"Hah! More the reverse. You break hearts and then take off without a word."

"Have I broken your heart?" he asked gently.

"A little," she said. "Did I break yours?"

"Definitely," he said. "It's only Scotch-taped together."

"Poor thing." She moved next to him and began kissing him tenderly all over. "Does that make it feel better? Does that help?"

"Much better," he said, surrendering himself to her kisses. "Much better."

10

Joel was reading aloud from a postcard:

" '. . . acres of oranges and olive trees stretch to the blue Mediterranean, and March here isn't like Paris. The Spanish sun is fantastic and there isn't a cloud in the sky.' "

He put it down. "He's going to Greece next."

"Screw you!" Laura said loudly, coming over to them. "*All* of you!"

They looked up at her, startled. Toni was sitting next to Melanie and Joel.

"Hi, Laura," Toni said.

"You all think I'm flaky," Laura said. "Just because I want to go to the medieval festival. Don't you?"

"Laura, are you drunk?" Melanie said.

"Drunk! Sure, the only reason I feel—oh, the

hell with it. I just came to tell you all I'm going. I'm leaving in two hours for Bourges. Despite all of *you!*"

"Laura, sit down!" Melanie said.

"No, thanks," Laura said haughtily. "I've got to go back to meet my friend."

They all looked at her blankly.

"Don't you want to know who my friend *is?*"

"Who's your friend, Laura?" Joel asked quietly.

"None of your damn business, Joel," Laura spat out. "He's a travel agent. I went to cancel my reservations—because I couldn't afford to go to the festival myself—and all of a sudden he said he'd take me."

"The travel agent?" Toni asked.

"His company was sending him," Laura said, "and his company will pay for the trip. I don't even have to pay for gas!"

Melanie was looking suspicious. "You just met this guy? Who *is* he?"

"And," Laura went on, oblivious, "he just took me to a real French restaurant for dinner and we had three wines, not like this dump," She looked scornfully at what they were eating.

"Is he French?" Melanie said.

"What? French?" Laura was startled for a moment. "I don't know," she admitted.

Sitting in the car next to Sayyid an hour later, she began feeling some qualms. I mean, after all, she didn't know this guy! What had she done? He was handsome and sauve and seemed nice, but he could have been an ax murderer, for all she knew!

Oh, come on. He worked for the agency. Would they employ an ax murderer? They might not know. He wouldn't tell them, after all. "I'd like this job because I just left Marseilles, where I was arrested for stuffing a woman in a post-office box . . ."

"How could you think I was French?" Sayyid said. "Me? Darius Sayyid, from the long line of the kings of Persia? I am Iranian! Where the haviar comes from."

"The what?" Laura said.

"You know. Haviar. Say it."

"Haviar," Laura said. "You mean caviar?"

He laughed. "No, haviar! It's so funny when you say it."

Laura got a funny feeling in her stomach. He was crazy! Oh no! "Listen, Sayyid," she said nervously. "Wouldn't we get there faster if we took the highway?"

"What? And miss the vineyards?"

That was true. He had pointed out that, without going out of their way, they could stop at some lovely vineyards and taste some of the best French wine. That would be something to write to David about! Laura sat back, trying to relax. And while all her dopey friends were scrounging away in Paris, studying, she would be sipping wine with . . . Sayyid, who was probably not an ax murderer at all, just a slightly crazy Iranian.

The wine was good. They sat and sipped. It was a lovely warm, sunny day. Laura glanced at Sayyid. What a pity she hated dark-haired men! If only he was David, thin and blond and intense looking. She squinted, trying to convert him into David in her imagination. He saw her looking at him and smiled. She was afraid he was getting drunk.

"You have a funny expression," he said.

"I do?"

"American women are so . . . mysterious." He finished his glass.

"Not me. I'm very straightforward."

"Oh no! Those green, emerald eyes . . . like a cat!"

"My eyes *aren't* emerald," Laura said. "They're—"

"The American woman," he went on, accepting more wine, "has hidden banks of sensuality, hidden deep *deep* within. The man who can awaken those fires—he is a lucky man!"

Oh, Jesus! Laura thought. I picked a real loony. "Hey, Sayyid," she said. "We've still got a long way to go."

"No problem," he said, weaving his way out of his seat. He smiled at her with his big black eyes. "Your hair is like spun gold," he said.

God, he must have read a lot of fourth-rate novels! "Thanks," she said curtly.

"I am enamored of blonds," he said, as they got back into the car. "Hair the color of gold, eyes the color of emeralds, skin white as . . . snow."

"Well," she said ironically, "I hope you find one, then."

He smiled enigmatically. "I have," he said.

In the car he drove with one hand on the wheel. Laura watched him nervously.

"I will tell you the big conflict in Sayyid's life," he said expansively. "You see, my religious background says: 'No, Sayyid, the liquid of the fermented grape must not touch your lips, but Sayyid loves the French wine. So what do I do?'"

"I don't know," Laura said, wishing he would keep his eyes on the road and stop referring to himself in the third person.

"I look deep into my heart and then I confess my problem to Allah. I pray and beg Allah, 'Please, Allah, give Sayyid a sign!' So what happens?"

Laura shrugged.

"Allah gives me a sign." The car swerved to one side.

"Maybe *I* should drive," Laura said.

He looked offended. "In my country, women do not drive."

"It figures," Laura said.

"In my country, in fact, the women run behind the cars." He laughed and glanced at her to see if she got the joke. "Sayyid joking," he said quickly, seeing her unamused face. "No problem. . . . Look! Another vineyard!"

"Sayyid, *no*, we're *not* stopping!" Laura said.

He turned the car off the road, judged badly, and hit a rock. They bounced down a ravine and crashed into the *Wine Tasting* sign, which flew into pieces and collapsed on top of the car. Sayyid looked stunned.

Laura glared at him. "You asshole!" she said.

She got up and removed the debris from the hood of the car. Sayyid stumbled off down the ravine to be sick. Laura got behind the wheel and waited for him. Christ almighty! What a wonderful beginning for a trip! Where had her judgment been? But he had seemed so nice at the restaurant and at the agency!

"I am all right now," he said, staggering back to the car, looking green. "I drive."

"You do *not* drive," Laura said firmly. "You *sit*. I drive."

She drove quickly and efficiently while he sat slumped beside her. I hope he doesn't throw up again, she thought. He stank slightly, which made her sick to her stomach. Oh, let us get there soon! Please!

When they arrived at the hotel, Laura stared in amazement. It was an ugly modern motel sprawling across an empty field. "*This* is where you booked our rooms?" she said in horror. "After all the beautiful chateaux we passed?"

"Too expensive," he said, miffed.

"The quaint little village inns we saw?"

"No vacancy."

"But this place?"

"No problem. Sayyid gets special discount."

They carried their bags down the hall. Laura looked around her in incomprehending dismay. What have I done to deserve this? she thought mournfully. Does *everything* have to turn out badly? It's not *fair!* "This is just a crummy motel," she said woefully. "We might as well be in Times Square!"

Sayyid gave her a big smile. "It's all new!" he

said cheerfully. "Why do you Americans only like *old* things? In *my* country we love everything modern."

Fuck his country! Why didn't he go back there and stay! She unlocked the door to her room. "I'm going to clean up," she said curtly, over her shoulder. "Then we'll go into town for the festival." At least there was the festival. At least she would get to see it *finally*. It wouldn't be a total loss.

In her room she showered. There was warm water. Getting out, she felt better. She dried her hair and sprinkled herself with cologne. Sitting on the edge of the bed, she sighed. Pull yourself together, she commanded. You can handle this.

Suddenly an adjoining door that she hadn't noticed opened. It was Sayyid.

"Surprise!" he said, "Sayyid feeling much better. I take shower. I recover."

"I feel better too," she admitted wryly. Of course, I didn't have as much to drink as you, you pig, she thought.

There was a knock at the door. "Wait! More surprise."

He opened the door. A waiter brought in a tray with a bottle of champagne, some glasses, and a small tin on it. Sayyid and the waiter conversed briefly in some unknown language. What did they speak in Iran anyway? Laura saw the waiter glance at her sidelong and then wink at Sayyid. Uh-oh! He darted out, closing the door behind them.

"What was *that* all about?" she said sardonically.

"Small world," Sayyid said. "We went to the same high school in Iran."

Sure. She watched as he opened the tin. "Haviar!" he exclaimed in delight.

"Caviar?" she said dubiously. "I've never had any."

"Haviar!" he insisted. He handed her some on a piece of toast. Laura took it and was about to bite into it when Sayyid swooped down and took her hand. He looked at her with his big, burning black eyes. "Sayyid is good to his women, isn't he?" he purred.

Laura gave him a shove. "Sayyid, cut it out, will you? I want to at least try haviar, okay?"

He was undaunted. He lunged at her and tried to take her in his arms. Laura looked at him in horror. "Listen, will you cut it *out!* What're you—*crazy?* I have a boyfriend in America, and even if I didn't, believe me, you're the last—"

He looked struck dumb with hurt and surprise. "But American girls do it with everyone," he said plaintively.

Laura shook her head. "What? Look, get out of my room, will you?" He made another lunge at her. "Let *go* of me! You've been around women in veils too long. In America we sleep with people we're attracted to, not any jackass that lunges at us!"

None of this seemed to make the least impression. Either he had an ego like a rock or he was totally and unbelievably insensitive. He tried to push her back on the bed. In desperation Laura grabbed the tin of caviar and shoved it in his face.

Hurray! Success! But even *that* didn't work. A second later he was up, fish eggs dripping from his cheeks. "I like infidel women!" he cried exultantly.

Laura threw everything at him—the ice, the toast. Then she made a mad dash for the door. Sayyid raced after her, but tripped on a lump of ice. In desperation he grabbed her leg. Laura felt herself hurtling across the floor. She thought in panic of the last scene of *Looking for Mr. Goodbar*. Her head crashed against the bureau; everything went black.

When she woke up, the room was dark. For a moment, she thought: Where am I? Oh my God, I don't know where I am! Then she remembered the whole scene. You were almost raped. Or was I raped? While I was unconscious? No, she could tell she hadn't been. He'd probably gotten scared when she slumped to the floor, and ducked out on her. Slowly, tentatively, Laura sat up. She clicked on a small bedside lamp. Her head hurt badly. She felt it. There was a big egg-shaped bump on one side. Look you're okay, she told herself. You passed out, which was just as well, and now you have a bump on your head, but you're okay. You weren't raped and you weren't murdered. Count your blessings.

The festival? It was nighttime. Had she missed it? Frantically she brushed her hair, slipped into her shoes, and ran downstairs. At the desk she asked, "Is the festival still on?"

"Festival?" said the Iranian at the desk.

"There's a medieval festival," Laura said, stuttering. "It's supposed to be—where's the main square? How do I get there?"

He gave her some confused directions. She hurried down the dark streets. The sidewalks were deserted. Where was everybody? What time was it? Finally she saw a lighted square in the distance. She crossed the street and started to run.

The square was empty. Only the remnants of the festival fluttered in the wind. Large wooden platforms were hung with torn crepe paper. Spotlights illuminated the cathedral. Laura walked around, unwilling to believe it was over. She walked up the steps of the cathedral and pulled on the door. It was locked. Slowly she went down the steps. The wind blew stray confetti at her. Balloons fluttered in the trees. It started to rain.

Then from somewhere she heard music. Turning, she saw light in a corner café. She hurried across the square. Inside the café she saw a man standing at the counter. Dressed in a bizarre medieval costume, he was having a beer and watching television. He turned and looked out at her. Laura moved away. She began to cry. It was as though someone else was crying. She felt the tears slipping down her cheeks and heard her own soft, rapid breathing, but it was as though it were happening to another person. The wind whipped rain across the square.

She walked to a bench and sat down in the rain, staring across at the square. I'm getting wet, she thought. I'm sitting in the rain getting wet. That isn't good. I might catch a cold. But it all seemed to come from a distance, as though the person thinking that and the actual person sitting there getting wet were two different people. I missed it, she thought. It's over. I'll never see it. I missed everything. With one hand she reached up and brushed her sodden hair out of her face. Her eyes were wet with tears and the rain; it was hard to see.

11

They were all gathered for a group portrait. Alex stood to one side, watching them: Toni, Melanie, Joel. He had gone to the institute first and been told he could find them there. It was the yearly picnic, someone had said. Alex hesitated. He felt depressed, and seeing everyone, seemingly in a gay, convivial mood, didn't help. He knew he needed a shave; he felt rumpled and disreputable looking. Look, just put on an act, he told himself. You're good at that. I am? Sure, go on. It's easy.

He found himself moving across the grass toward his friends. A frisbee glided over his head.

Joel was taking a photo of Toni. He turned in surprise when he saw Alex. "Hey, I thought you were in Greece!"

Alex kissed Toni. "I didn't get that far."

"How was your trip?" Toni asked.

"It was great," Alex said with false heartiness.

"So why'd you come back?" Melanie said.

Alex shrugged. "Well, I've got to refuel. I'm hoping for some cash from home."

Joel made a wry face. "Don't count on it. You can't imagine the uproar after you left. The letters and phone calls! Your parents went beserk when you dropped out."

Alex sighed. "Well, I had to do it. It was necessary. . . . I went by the institute and it looked closed down."

"No such luck," Joel said. "We've been slaving away."

"There *have* been some minor changes," Melanie said. She nodded toward Madame Tessier, who was talking with Christine. "Monsieur Tessier is no longer with us. She's running the place by herself now."

Alex felt his heart start beating rapidly at the sight of her. "I'm sure she'll be very successful," he said stiffly. He watched her get into her car and drive off.

"You know, if we're going to drop by the hospital, we better get going," Melanie said.

"Hospital?" Alex said. "Who's sick?"

Joel looked uncomfortable. "It's Laura. She had a kind of . . . well, breakdown."

Alex looked concerned. "Really? How did it happen?"

"She went to that festival—you know, the one she was always talking about?" Melanie said, "—with this really weird guy, this Iranian travel

162

agent, and well, I guess he tried to rape her or something and she kind of freaked out."

"Jesus," Alex said.

"She's going to be all right, I think," Joel said. "She was just kind of shaken up."

"She's had a bad year," Toni said sympathetically.

"Well, it was her own fault in a way," Melanie said. "I kept telling her to stop mooning around after David all the time. She was just using him like a crutch. She never got *involved* in anything over here. I wasn't surprised, frankly, that it happened."

"Can I come—to the hospital?" Alex said. "I'd like to."

"Sure ... We might as well go now, actually."

On the way to the hospital Alex kept thinking of Madame Tessier. The trip had been a failure as an attempt to get over her. He'd thought of her constantly, in every romantic setting he was in, had relived each moment of their time together, replayed it with different endings, no plane strike. In Nice he'd looked out at the Mediterranean and imagined the two of them in summertime, lying on the beach, she in a skimpy bikini, soaking up the sun. At every small roadside inn in Brittany he thought of their sharing one of those rooms with the big beds covered by soft, downy comforters, lace curtains at the window, a view of the sea outside, gray and cool. They could have taken a long drive in Aix en Provence, the windows of the car open, the wind blowing in fresh smells, her hair loose, the tall trees arching along the road, that scent of sun and grass and cool clay.

Shit, it had been a lousy trip, he'd thrown away a year of credit, for what? Joel had been right not to go.

The hospital room was very bare except for a crucifix hanging on the wall. Laura was lying in bed, the sheet pulled up to her neck. When they came in, she sat up slowly. She looked pale and fragile, a tentative expression on her face.

"Hi," Melanie said heartily. "I brought some visitors."

"Hi," Toni said. "You look better."

"Alex just came back from Spain," Melanie said.

Laura looked at him, her eyes questioning. "Was it nice?" she said. "I went on a . . . trip too. Only it didn't turn out that well. I—" Suddenly she broke down and started to cry.

Alex frowned. He wanted to go over and comfort her, but didn't know how.

"Oh, God, don't start crying already," Melanie said impatiently. "We just got here." She reached into her purse. "Look, here—some goodies. A letter from David—"

Laura took the letters and put them in her lap. A severe-looking nurse entered the room and gave them all the evil eye, then exited. "They don't like me to get excited," Laura said in a soft, even voice. "At first they thought I had pneumonia from sitting out in the rain, but now I guess they think it's . . . some kind of breakdown." It obviously was hard for her to say that.

"Do they give you any medicine?" Alex asked, trying to sound sympathetic.

She made a wry face. "Oh, God, for two weeks they had me on something—it must have been Thorazine or something like that. All I did was sleep! I guess they just wanted me to be under."

"That's stupid!" Alex said angrily. "I had a friend who had a breakdown, and they gave him all that stuff. He said it was worse than being sick."

"Well," she said thoughtfully, "maybe it wasn't so bad, being out of it for a while. It was sort of peaceful in a way. It's coming out of it that isn't so . . ." Her voice trailed off. "Hey, you know this is one of France's oldest and most famous hospitals, did you know that? Baudelaire died of syphilis here!"

"Hopefully in another room," Melanie said dryly. "Hey, listen, I've got to go. Jean-Claude said he'd meet me at five."

"We should too," Joel said, taking Toni's hand. "We'll see you in a couple of days, okay, Laura?"

"Sure," she said tentatively. "Thanks for coming, all of you."

Alex found himself alone in the room with her. He stood there uncomfortably, not knowing what to say. "I'm sorry I'm dressed this way," he said finally. "I just got back today."

"You look nice," she said wistfully. "It's nice that you came. I feel . . . well, embarrassed. I guess. Pneumonia would be easier to talk about. This is a little scary."

"You feel better now?"

"Well, yes." She frowned. "The thing is, I've had a lot of time to think, being here, and I realize, I've just realized a lot of things about myself that maybe I didn't want to know. I mean, I think I *was* using David, really, while I was here, because I didn't want to get involved in anything. That's the story of my life, kind of, always studying. Even the thing with him. Leaping into it, using it as a . . . way of not facing life."

"Why do you think you didn't want to face life?" Alex asked.

She looked at him. She has beautiful eyes, he thought. "I don't know," she said with a smile. "It's complicated. I guess I'm that kind of person. Oh, there's still a lot I have to figure out, but I feel like—I'm not so scared anymore . . . It's just ironical. Here this was supposed to be this great year. I remember getting off the plane in Paris and thinking—you know that dumb thing you see on bumper stickers?—'This is going to be the first day of the rest of your life'— And then it was just a . . . nightmare."

Alex sighed. "Well, that's exactly what happened to me! First this stupid thing with Madame Tessier—"

"But I thought you—I thought she—"

"No, when her husband showed up, it was clear she was just using me, fooling around." He tried not to sound too bitter. "So I raced off on this dumb trip and had a shitty time, lost all my credits, I'll have to do the whole damn *year* over. Jesus!"

"I'm sorry, Alex," Laura said. "I didn't know."

"I didn't tell them," he said, "about the trip, I mean. I just pretended it was this great thing. I had a terrific time. Ha! It was a total nightmare, like what you said."

She smiled. "Well, this thing with my Iranian friend—"

"Did he really try to rape you?"

"Yeah. It was like, did you ever see that movie *Looking for Mr. Goodbar?*"

"Un-uh."

"Well, that was about this girl who supposedly—she really *liked* creeps, so finally she met up with one who killed her. . . . But ironically, I'm not like that. I always liked boys who were— well, nice. I guess I just had bad judgment. I wanted to go to the festival and no one would go with me, so I just figured here was this guy who seemed friendly . . . Little did I know."

"I'm really sorry," Alex said. "That must have been awful."

"Well, I'm not scarred for life or anything. I was just—"

"Did you write David about it?"

She shook her head. "I don't think I will . . . Do you think that's cowardly?"

"Well, not cowardly maybe, but—"

"The thing is, it doesn't have anything to do with him and—I don't know, I can't explain it. I just don't want him to know."

"I understand," Alex said, not positive he did.

"Do you?" Her face lit up. "You know, it's been so good talking to you, Alex, I mean it. I couldn't talk about this with anyone. I felt so lousy. I really feel better now."

He smiled. He felt good, hearing her say that. "Well, listen, I'm going to be around for a few days . . . Do you mind if I come back and visit you?"

"No, that would be great . . . The thing is, I'm getting out over the weekend."

"Well, I'll see you, then . . ." He stood, gazing at her reflectively. "I think you're different from most girls I've known."

She flushed. "I am? How?"

"Well, you're so open about everything."

"All women are," she said breathlessly.

"No, they're not, far from it. It's pretty rare, if you come down to it. I think a lot of girls and women just like manipulating men for their own ends."

Laura looked puzzled. "Really? Do you think so? I thought that was only a cliché."

"Well, it seems to have some basis in reality. Listen, I don't know. I haven't . . . known that many girls or women or whatever, but it just seems . . . you never know where you stand or why they're doing what or anything!"

Laura laughed. "Poor thing."

He smiled. "Well, I've survived so far."

"You'll survive. Don't worry."

"Okay, I won't."

Later, Alex thought about Laura. He remembered that first day on the bus and overhearing her tentative comments to Melanie about David. "You must like the introspective type . . . True love."

She was sensitive. Would she like him? Was *he* her type? Was she even looking for anyone after that horrible thing with the Iranian? And he remembered that conversation in the museum where she had berated herself for taking everything so seriously and he had offered to take her to the movies. He let his mind wander dreamily. They were in bed, she was lying there. He loved her hair, that long, thick blond hair. What would she look like naked? She was a little heavy. Not fat, but well rounded, full hips. She would be beautiful. Shit. Fuck David. He's probably making it with ten girls by now, and she . . .

He remembered the conversation they had had, that intense, almost breathless way she had of talking, her eyes fixed on him as though he were the only person in the world. That's just her manner. It's not you. He fantasied going to her and saying, "Laura, we've both had a terrible year. Let's have a terrific year from now on. We can just . . ." He imagined them making love, her greenish eyes looking up at him, the blond hair spread out on the pillow, that tentative, almost frightened expression she sometimes got. "I thought it was good with David, but you . . ."

Damn! Cut it out! Where did all that get you with Madame Tessier? Nowhere.

12

"There were some interesting things about the trip," Alex said. He was strolling with Laura along the Seine. She had gotten out of the hospital the day before. "I saw a bullfight. I watched a horse get gored."

"Ugh."

"Yeah, it was . . . well, I guess I'm not the Hemingway type."

"I should hope not!" she said indignantly, at the thought that he might insult himself that way.

"I picked up my plane ticket today," he went on. He was wearing a vest over his shirt. She liked that.

"You have to leave?" Laura said, trying not to sound disappointed.

"I'd stay, but I'm out of money. My parents finally pulled the plug. So I'm going home Tuesday.

Remember in the hospital how you were talking about your great expectations for this year?"

She nodded sadly. "What did you *think* the year was going to be like?"

He shrugged. "I don't know. I thought . . . I guess I hoped it would be—" His voice trailed off. Suddenly he reached down and took her hand. Laura looked up at him curiously. A moment later he turned back to her, away from the boat on the shimmering water floating down the river, the crimson clouds on the horizon, the fishermen on the Île Saint-Louis watching their lines. "You know, I kind of hoped that the year was going to be . . . like this." He bent down and kissed her.

It was a long, tender, romantic kiss. Laura felt herself hesitate, and then decided— What the hell. She kissed him back. It was a good, a wonderful feeling. His lips were warm. When they broke apart, he said nervously, "Listen, I—I'm sorry."

"Why?"

"Well, you just got out of the hospital and maybe—"

"That doesn't matter," Laura said firmly. "Look what got me *into* the hospital. Being afraid of everything. Afraid of life, afraid of love. I'm not going to *be* like that anymore!" She felt defiant.

He was frowning; he looked uncertain. "The thing is, I know this sounds stupid and it probably is, but I have the feeling I'm falling in love with you."

Laura swallowed. She took a deep breath. "Well,

172

that's okay," she said, not looking at him. "I think maybe I'm falling in love with *you* too."

"You *are?*" He looked delighted.

"Yeah, well . . . You were so nice and sympathetic and everything in the hospital, and then I've always, well, I always thought you were extremely good-looking and everything."

"You did?"

She decided to confess everything. She told him how she had been planning to sleep with him and was going to tell Joel to tell him she found him attractive.

"I can't *believe* it," Alex said. "You mean, that time I met you at the museum—"

She nodded. "The thing was, you seemed so . . . entranced or whatever with Madame Tessier, I decided it wasn't such a great idea."

Alex shook his head. "Oh God. I wish you'd told him! Christ, all this never needed to have happened. I didn't need to have gone on that dumb trip to Spain and you wouldn't have had the breakdown."

"Well," Laura said slowly, "I don't know if for me the breakdown was such a bad thing, really. You see, I feel maybe it showed I wasn't living the right way, it was a sign."

"What was wrong with the way you'd been living?"

"I was hiding from life, I was scared of everything. What if this happens and what if that happens? What if David finds another girl, what if I'm attracted to someone else? . . . And the thing is, so *what?* That's life! Life is being hurt and taking chances, it isn't hiding in a little corner with a blanket pulled over your head."

"Joel says sort of the same thing," Alex said, "that till this year, till the thing with Toni, he never *did* anything, he just listened to other people tell about their adventures."

"That's the story of my *life*," Laura said. "Look at the thing with Melanie. Practically since I was *six,* I've had best friends like that who were always out screwing with boys. In college my roommate used to moan on and on about when was I going to finally sleep with someone, because she wanted to talk about orgasms with someone. She used to print these big signs in red ink saying: 'Sensuality,' 'Aggression,' the mottoes for the month. And there I was, scared to go to the *library* because boys were there! . . . When I finally met David, I think she was relieved. She was afraid I'd never lose my virginity till I was eight hundred or something."

"Do you think you really . . . loved him?" Alex said tentatively. "Love him, I mean?"

Laura gazed at him reflectively. "I don't know, Alex. Isn't that funny? Maybe it wasn't love at all. He was nice and smart and tall and thin and he liked me. That seemed like love, then, but if we saw each other now, I just don't know. I feel like I'm a different person than I was before."

"Me too."

"Did you have a girl friend back home?" she said, trying to be bold.

He shrugged. "Not really . . . There was some-

174

one I saw, but it wasn't anything much. I guess being in Paris sort of . . . well, it makes you start acting in kind of a crazy way."

She smiled at him. Suddenly, to her own amazement, she found herself saying, "Do you want to make love?"

Alex looked at her, startled. "You mean in general, or right now?"

"Right now."

"Well—uh—sure . . . Are you sure you—do you really want to?"

"Yeah, I really do . . . Do you want to go to your place or mine?"

"I guess ours would be all right. Joel is never there anymore because of Toni."

"Okay, let's go there, then."

He seemed stunned by her proposal and just walked quietly by her side, holding her hand. She was a little stunned too. It must be done, she thought. You started it and you have to go ahead with it.

She loooked around the room. It was messy, the bed unmade. Alex began trying to straighten it up. "I never thought anyone would come here," he said. "I'm sorry."

"That's okay," Laura said. She looked at him. "Should I take my clothes off or would you rather take them off?"

"I think I—maybe I could help you," he said, still with that almost frightened look on his face. He came over and began unbuttoning her dress. "That's a really pretty dress," he said.

"Do you like it?" She felt pleased. "I thought it would make me look—sort of French, sort of sophisticated."

"It does."

"The horrible thing," she confessed, "is, I've gained ten *pounds* over here, and I should have *lost* five. The trouble is, when I get depressed, I eat."

"You look fine to me," he said.

"Don't look too hard," she warned. "All the French women look so thin! I think they shoot women who weigh more than a hundred and thirty." The dress, unbuttoned, slipped to the floor. Under it she was wearing just a bra and pantyhose. "I'm sorry I don't have sexy underwear," she apologized. "The thing is, I didn't really expect this to happen."

"That's okay," he said. His hands were trembling slightly as he unhooked the bra, it hooked in the front. He let his hands move over her breasts; he kissed her. She could feel his heart pounding as they stood close. "God, you're so beautiful!" he gasped.

Laura smiled at him. "No, I'm not," she said. "Alex, you don't have to make up stuff to me, really. It's not necessary."

He was frowning, almost in disbelief. "You're *beautiful*," he said, so intensely that it was clear he really meant it. He began talking his clothes off hurriedly. Laura stood gazing at him. He had a nice body. He was shorter and less muscular than David; there wasn't much hair on his chest, but he had long slim legs and a narrow waist.

"You have a nice body," she said politely. She wasn't sure if men wanted you to comment on things like that.

He smiled. "Thank you," he said. He took her hand and led her to the bed.

"I wish I weighed ten pounds less," she couldn't resist saying.

"Laura, listen," Alex said. "You're beautiful just the way you are! Think of Rubens and Renoir and just about anyone you can name."

"True," Laura said, not really convinced. "That was a while back, though."

They lay down side by side, gazing at each other. Alex ran his hand down her hip. "You're nicely rounded, that's all," he said, leaning over to kiss her.

"Okay, if you say so." Now that they were there together, she didn't feel nervous anymore, which surprised her; she felt amazingly calm. They kissed and caressed each other, and when he entered her, it seemed all perfectly natural, as though they had been doing this for ages and knew everything there was to know about each other. For a moment, in the middle, she had a second of fright. This isn't David, she thought. I'm doing it with someone other than David. What if I have an orgasm? What would David say? Forget about David, some other voice intruded. Just forget about everything but this, this is all that matters. That voice prevailed, and she gave herself to what was happening and it was wonderful.

When it was over, she lay there quietly, leaning

against him. "That was really good," she said finally. "Thank you."

He smiled. "Thank *you*," he said.

Laura looked up at the ceiling with its ornate decoration. "You know, I think we deserve this in a way, don't you? I mean, we both had such a lousy year. Why should't we have a little fun?"

"My sentiments exactly," Alex said.

"Are you still planning to go away in a few days?"

"Not if I can help it."

"Maybe we can think of something, a way you can stay. . . . I would feel sort of shitty if you went away."

He pulled her into his arms. "I'm not going to go away," he said. "I may be dumb, but not *that* dumb."

* * *

Outside Madame Tessier's office, Laura felt nervous. Finally she screwed up her courage and walked in. Madame Tessier was sitting behind her desk, looking over some papers.

"It's about Alex," she said. "You know, he came back and—"

"Yes, I saw him," Madame Tessier said, looking at her coolly.

"The thing is," Laura said, "I wondered if you could give him, like, you know, a second chance? He'd really work hard to catch up."

"I doubt it," Madame Tessier said.

"He would!" Laura said earnestly. "Really. He's turned over a new leaf completely. . . . See, the thing is, before, he was in love with you and that kept him from studying, but now he's a completely new person, now that—"

"—now that you and he are sleeping together." Madame Tessier finished her sentence.

Laura swallowed. "Well, yeah."

"I am quite prepared to believe that having an adequate sex partner may lend a certain stability to Alex's life," Madame Tessier said, "but the fact is, he is *disastrously* behind. It is just not *possible* for him to catch up."

"Couldn't you give him a chance?" Laura said. Suddenly an inspiration hit her. "The thing is, if he went home and told everyone about everything that went on here with the teachers and students, it might not be such great publicity for the institute."

Madame Tessier stared at her, obviously trying to psych out how much Laura knew. After a moment she said, "All right. Alex can finish the year. He can borrow lecture notes from other students. But he has to remember there will be no allowance made for this absence. Finals are coming soon and—"

"Oh, he'll study," Laura said happily. "Thanks so much, Madame Tessier. That's really terrific!"

"It was nothing," Madame Tessier said calmly, returning to her papers.

Outside, Alex was sitting in the lounge, playing some aimless notes on the piano. Laura ran over and hugged him. "I did it!" she exclaimed. "You're back in!"

He stood up and hugged her. "Great . . . How'd you convince her?"

Laura gave him a mischievous smile. "Oh, I used a few little . . . feminine wiles. I decided when in Rome and all that."

"You're terrific," he said.

"I think she still has a crush on you," Laura said.

Alex turned red. "Why do you think that?"

"Oh, I don't know, something about her manner. Well, listen, she doesn't have anybody, now that old sourpuss took off. She probably regrets booting you out that way. Well, tough! It's too late . . . So, do I get a reward for my good deed?"

He bent down and kissed her. "There. How's that?"

"A good *hors d'oeuvre*," Laura said. "Now how about the main course?"

Laughing, he walked out with his arm around her. Laura looked up, to see Madame Tessier watching them pensively. For a second she felt sorry for her. She's lonely, she thought. And then she thought. Too bad. That's her problem. She had *her* chance.

13

Toni was lying on the bed, looking at the slides he had taken of her. Joel sat at the typewriter, pecking away. He'd never learned to touch-type, but could go pretty fast with two fingers. He was writing the play for the institute students to put on at the end of the year. Acts one and two were finished. Act three was giving him some trouble. He'd redone it three times already.

"What are these pictures?" Toni asked.

"They're for the play," Joel said.

"I thought you had to study for finals."

He kept on typing. "You think Ionesco studied for finals?"

"When did you take these pictures of me?" she exclaimed suddenly. "You can't keep these!"

She pulled the slide out. Joel grabbed for it. They fought over the slide, rolling on the bed.

"You're *not* leaving this country with these!" Toni said. "Customs will arrest you."

He kissed her. "I want to remember how beautiful you are. I want to look at those every day so I can believe it really happened and wasn't just a fantasy." He sighed. "There's so little time left."

She looked pensive. "I know!"

He smiled. "But I shall return—next summer. Until then I'll write you long, passionate letters."

She raised an eyebrow. "Sure, then the letters will slow down. And by next summer the closest you will get to coming back here is when you show these pictures and some other girl asks, maybe a little jealous, 'Who is the French girl?' and to impress her you'll say, 'Oh, that's just a girl I once knew in Paris.' "

He was silent a moment. "I'm not that kind of person," he said finally.

She snorted. "All men are the same."

"How can you say such a stupid thing?" he said. "Is that what you think I'm like, some blockhead like Steven?"

"Well . . ."

"It's just as likely, more so, that *you'll* forget *me*," he said. "Another bunch of Americans off the plane, you wander down to the institute, someone smiles at you—"

"Jealousy is an undignified emotion," she said coolly.

"Sure," he said, "so if I go to bed with a dozen girls and it's terrific with all of them, you won't care, right?"

"Not unless you fall in love with one of them."

"Maybe I will," he said defiantly.

"I thought you were planning on lifelong fidelity."

"Not if you're not."

"Joel, I'm not *like* you. What happens, happens. You can't plan ahead."

"Sure you can!" he said angrily. "You can make a commitment and stick to it. To *me* that means something."

"It means something *now*," she said. "But you can't tell how you'll feel when you meet someone you haven't even . . . met yet."

"I can," he said stubbornly. "I *can* tell."

"You lie to yourself," she said sadly. "That is the saddest kind of lying of all."

"If I swear to you I won't touch another girl, I won't," he said.

"Maybe."

"Christ, you're so cynical!"

"Perhaps I've simply seen more of the world than you."

"Well, if all it's done is turn you into a cynic at twenty, that's pretty pathetic."

She smiled and leaned over and ruffled his hair. "The great romantic," she said.

"Stop making fun of me!" He pulled away.

Her voice became tender. "Joel, I'm *not*. But you take everything so seriously!"

"Being in love *is* serious for me," he said. "Isn't it for you?"

"Yes," she said after a moment.

"Nothing more serious than that has ever happened to me. I'm not going to be able to think of anything but you all year long! Even when I'm sitting there, typing, all I can think about is you!"

"You have a bad case," she said teasingly.

"Fatal," he said. "Hey, listen, I have a sudden terrific unconfessable urge."

"Yes? Something new? Something we never did before?"

"Yes." He leaned over and whispered in her ear. "I want to go to McDonald's."

Toni burst out laughing. "Joel, you are truly crazy, you know that?"

"It's just a momentary lapse," he said. "Actually I prefer steak tartare and *coquilles Saint-Jacques,* but I suddenly felt I had to bite into a nice, thick, rubbery, tasteless American-style hamburger or I'd die."

She sat in the McDonald's watching him eat with a kind of wonderment. "This is what you call . . . junk food?"

"Precisely . . . No vitamins, no nutrition, total junk." He took another bite happily. "How come you're not eating?"

"I'm still thinking about our conversation," she confessed, "about you leaving."

Joel thought a minute. "You know, I just had what is probably the most brilliant inspiration of my life."

"Two in one evening?"

"No, this is real genius. . . . It will sound crazy,

184

but it's not . . . Why don't you come back to America with me?"

She frowned. "What do you mean?"

"Listen, I have the whole thing planned. There are lots of little orchestras in New York. You're good. You could study and work at night. My parents go to this chamber music group at the Metropolitan Museum called Musica Aeterna, and my mother is always saying that one thing she likes about it is that it has about half women. You could try out for that."

Toni sighed. "Am I good enough?"

"You know you are . . . And you could keep studying. New York has the best flute teachers in the world." He didn't know if it was true, but it sounded like it might be. "Anyhow, if you're worried about work permits and stuff, we can just get married."

"You're crazy!"

"I don't mean *married* married," he said hastily. "Just an arrangement so you can stay in the country. People do that all the time. It'd be fun."

"Joel, have you thought about this?"

"Yeah, sure. Just now."

"I just can't go like that," Toni protested. "It's not that easy."

"No, you're wrong," Joel said intensely, staring at her. "I used to do that—worry about everything. Life's too short. This is the new Joel you're looking at. If you want to do something, you just do it."

Toni was gazing at him with a thoughtful, amused expressed, as though torn between taking him seriously and regarding the whole thing as a joke.

"So, what do you say?" Joel said. He reached out and took her hand. "Really. I'd like you to go back with me. Should I put it more romantically?" He gestured. "I'm madly in love with you and nothing in the world would make me happier than if you said you'd come."

"You're serious?"

"Absolutely . . . *You* know me. I'm *always* serious."

"We could be making a terrible mistake."

"So, we'll get divorced."

She frowned. "But marriage . . . That *is* serious. I don't know if I'm . . . ready."

"So, who's ready? You think *I* am?"

"What would our parents say?"

"They'll freak out totally. They'll disown us."

She burst out laughng. "Joel, you're so funny."

"All we'll have is each other. It'll really be romantic. No money, no jobs, just love."

"It's such a totally impractical proposal, I'm tempted to accept."

"Accept!" he said. "Come on, here I am, falling at your feet, besotted by love—"

She was still smiling affectionately. "Yes, but Joel, you know *nothing* about women. I'm your first. Ten years from now you'll think: 'I should have waited, I should have tried others.' "

"Ten years from now I may be dead."

She looked alarmed. "Dead! Why?"

"No, I just mean anything can happen. Who

186

knows about ten years from now? Right now I love you and you love me. So what else matters?"

"The last of the romantics," she said.

"Right. Here I am. The last specimen of a dying species . . . I'll bring you flowers, I'll never forget your birthday, I'll take you out on our anniversary to wonderful restaurants, I'll write you terrible lyric poetry about how lovely you are, I'll carry a nude photo of you in my wallet so I can stare at it during the day . . ."

She sighed. "What am I going to do? I love you, it's true. I don't know why, I never expected to fall in love with someone like you, I didn't even know anyone like you existed . . . until I met you."

"No one like me *does* exist . . . except me," he said, smiling.

"What about *me?*" she said. "I'm worried about me. What if I conceive a grand passion for someone else?"

"I'll shoot you, both of you. A crime of passion. I'll go to jail and write my memoirs."

"Joel, please be serious."

"Toni, you will *never* be unfaithful to me. I'll make love to you so wonderfully every night that you won't have any time or inclination to think of another man."

She smiled. "I believe you."

"I'll change my personality every five years so you won't get bored."

"Will we have children? A real marriage?"

"Definitely . . . First we'll have a little girl who will look just like you, with big eyes and long eyelashes, and I'll carry her piggyback and fall madly in love with her. Then we can have a little boy—"

"—who looks like you, for me to flirt with?"

"Right . . . We'll take them to the park on Sunday and all the other husbands will look at you and be jealous of me and I'll beam in a self-satisfied way and read *The New York Times*."

"And I will have a job in a small orchestra?"

"Yes. I'll sit in the audience and watch you playing the flute and nudge people and say, 'Do you see that beautiful woman in the black dress who plays the flute so beautifully? That's my wife!' And I'll applaud louder than anyone else and yell 'Bravo' when you do a solo and people will stare at me and say, 'It's his wife, he can't help it.' "

"What if I hadn't met you?" she said suddenly. "None of this would have happened."

"No, we *had* to meet," he said seriously. "It's all been charted out. We were doomed to meet. Someone was sitting up there with a big book and he said, 'Let's see. We have one shy, lonely Jewish intellectual. He's had a pretty boring life. Let's toss him a lovely, petite, sexy French girl and see how he'll handle that.' See, *they* thought I'd screw it up, *they* didn't think I could handle it. They were wrong."

"Okay," Toni said. "I agree. I will do it."

Joel grinned from ear to ear. He waved his hand at the waiter. "*Garçon, encore* two Big Macs, *s'il vous plaît!* Isn't my French getting terrific?"

She leaned over and kissed him tenderly on the lips. "*Everything* about you is terrific," she said.

14

Alex stared straight ahead. The day of decision had come. They were about to receive the results of their final exams. Madame Tessier was sitting at the head of the room with five professors next to her, glaring out at the students like a military junta.

"Along with your corrected examinations," she was saying, "you will find your final grades for your courses. If you have any questions, I'm sure that your professors will be more than happy to discuss them with you."

The institute staff was walking down the aisle, handing out the blue books. Alex took his, but didn't have the courage to open them. He had studied frantically, but he wasn't sure it had been enough to make up for all the time away.

"How did you do?" Laura whispered.

"I'm scared to open them."

She gave him a dirty glance, took his blue books, and looked inside. "Well, what do you know? You passed Nineteenth Century Novel! Soule gave you a C." She opened another. "An A from Madame Tessier? What's that for? An A for—"

Alex snatched the blue books from her and stared down at the page. There it was, a big red A. He smiled. "Well, I guess, credit where credit is due. No hard feelings." He glanced at Madame Tessier, but she was talking to another student. A! He didn't deserve an A. Why had she given it to him? Because she still . . . Cut it out! That's over. He knew Laura was looking at him.

"Fuck her," Laura said.

"Look, I studied hard for that exam."

"Sure."

"You *know* I did."

"I know you didn't deserve an A and so do you."

He sighed. "Look, she's trying to make it up to me for—"

"For what? For not fucking with you when she had the chance?"

He shrugged. "I don't know."

"Alex, I am warning you, if she goes after you, there is going to be big trouble."

He laughed nervously. "What makes you think she'll go after me?"

"I've seen her give you those sidelong sexy glances. The second you're out of my sight, she's going to—"

"You're imagining the whole thing."

"Bullshit . . . She's just waiting for the right moment. And if you so much as—"

"Laura, I told you, it's over. I have *no* feeling for her whatever. None."

"Cut it out! What were you doing one second ago goggling her, then?"

"I wasn't goggling her!"

"You were *so!* Every time you look at her, you get this sick, moping expression."

He blushed. "I do?"

"Yes, damn it . . . And I'm just telling you, I am a *very* insecure person. I'm *extremely* jealous, and I don't want *any* monkey business. Fantasize all you like, but leave it at that."

"Believe me, even if I—which I don't—she just—"

"Alex! What was *that?* 'Even if I—' "

He shook his head. "Laura, listen, she's beautiful, she did . . . turn me on. It's true, it hasn't all totally vanished, but I feel a loyalty to you."

She frowned. "Do you?"

"Sure."

She was silent a moment. "That's nice of you."

"It's not a matter of niceness. I *love* you. What I felt for her was . . . I don't know. Some crazy mixture of lust, romance—"

"Crazy," Laura repeated thoughtfully.

"Crazy . . . She's fifteen years older than me. I was flattered that she even was willing to *look* at me—"

"To say nothing of—"

"She was lonely, he was treating her like shit, I

was available, I'd been trailing her around all year. It wasn't that she was madly in love with me."

Laura looked morose. "You're good-looking, you're young, you have a great body . . . She just wanted to make it with you, that's all!"

He felt flattered. "Nothing's going to happen, okay?"

"You don't feel you have to reward her for giving you an A?"

"Absolutely not."

She sighed. "Okay, I believe you, I'm trusting you, okay? So be trustworthy."

He took her hand. "I will. I promise."

Suddenly Joel came rushing up. He'd been hysterical ever since rehearsals for the play had started. Alex was going to play the piano and sing a few songs. "We've got to go over to the auditorium now!" Joel said excitedly.

Alex stood up. "I've got to check on something first."

"Where are you going?" Laura asked.

"I'll see you tonight," Alex said. "It's a surprise. I'll tell you later."

Joel grabbed his sleeve. "Hey, Alex, you can't desert me *now*. What about the music?"

"I'll be at the auditorium by five. Relax, pal."

"Relax! He says to relax! This is the biggest moment of my *life*. My first play!"

"It's going to be a big success, Joel," Laura said reassuringly. "Don't worry."

"I *have* to worry. It's my nature."

"I'll see you both later," Alex said. "So long."

He wanted to make it up to Laura, but actually he'd had the plan for several days now. Now that exams were over, they could go together to Greece. They would take the trip he'd wanted to take, but they'd be together. No more worries, no studying. Just long lunches with wine and feta cheese and Greek olives and making love all afternoon . . .

That evening he went backstage. Laura was getting into her costume. She was going to do a song-and-dance routine. Her hair was frizzed out in a funny way. She looked sexy and cute, but not like herself.

He waved the brochures at her.

"Greece?" she said. "Well, sure I'd like to go to Greece, but—"

"That's what I was checking on," he said excitedly. "I found out if we cash in our return plane tickets—"

"How do we get home?"

"You don't want to go home, do you? We'll worry about that later. We've got the summer, and if we take the train third-class, hitchhike—"

"You're forgetting about our last trips," Laura said wryly.

"Yes, but this time we'll be together."

She smiled. "Listen, if Greece hears we're coming together, they'll close the country. . . . Alex, will you get out of here? I've got to—"

"Just say yes and I'll go."

"Importuning me, are you?"

"Right . . . Think of it. Long hot afternoons, making love till we pass out—"

She laughed. "Sounds tempting."

"It'll be fantastic. Something to remember next winter when we're studying our heads off."

"I don't even want to *think* of next winter," she said.

"Why? I'll be seeing you every other weekend."

"You will *not!* Alex, come on, be sensible. This is a classic shipboard-romance type thing."

"Who's on board ship?"

"*You* know what I mean. It's Paris, we're young, the whole schmeer . . . Back in the States—"

"Nope, sorry, this is just the beginning of—"

"What? True love?"

He nodded seriously. "Yes."

"Look, you're getting me *terribly* rattled."

"Just say yes."

"To what? True love? Greece?"

"Right, both."

"Okay, yes. . . . Now scram." She gave him a shove.

He left.

* * *

Joel felt frantic. He was trying to direct his assistants, who were manning a slide projector and tape recorder. Toni was standing next to him.

"I looked at the audience," she said. "I think they like it."

"That's because they like to see people humiliated," Joel said mournfully. "Thank God we're leaving the country tomorrow."

"You're still sure you want me to go with you?"

"We've been through all that. Of course I'm sure. It's all planned and there's nothing in the world that's going to change—oh my God!"

It was his parents. His mother rushed over, arms outstretched, and embraced him.

"Joel, we've missed you!"

He felt stunned. "Shh, quiet down, my play's . . . Jesus, what're you *doing* here?"

She beamed. "It's a surprise. We've arranged it so we can all spend our vacation together."

"We're taking you to Finland with us tomorrow," his father said.

"Finland?" He was horror-struck.

"And Lapland!"

"Lapland? . . . Listen, why don't you and Dad go get a seat in front and . . . Toni, wait! Don't go away!" He raced after her.

She looked furious. "You didn't even tell your parents we were going back together! You are a lily-livered coward!"

Joel felt terribly flustered. "I'm going to tell them tonight. Listen, I'm in a state of shock. They never said they were coming over. Lapland! My God!"

"They will steal you away," she said severely, arms crossed.

"They will *not* steal me away. I'm not a baby. Sweetie, give me a chance, will you? I feel like I'm coming apart at the seams."

"I'm *not* your sweetie. Don't call me that."

"You *are!* Now listen, I can't take any more anxiety right now. My anxiety quotient is up to a hundred and ten. So please!"

She sighed. "Okay."

He kissed her. "I love you . . . God, why did they *do* this to me? Finland! Lapland!"

* * *

Offstage Laura stood breathless, exhilarated by the applause. She thought her cabaret number had gone well. Then she glanced to one side. Madame Tessier was standing there, eyes fixed on Alex, who was on stage playing the rinky-tink piano. She had a kind of mesmerized stare, as though she were hypnotized. Laura felt as though she'd been socked in the stomach. She took a deep breath and walked over to her.

"You should be out in the audience, Madame Tessier," she said brightly. "You'd have a better view."

Madame Tessier glanced at her. She was wearing a very sexy long-sleeved black dress; she looked fantastic. Laura felt totally outclassed. "I have to talk to Alex before he leaves," she said.

"Oh yeah? Why?"

Madame Tessier got a dreamy look. "I've just been thinking about him . . . since he came back to me."

Laura stared at her. "To *you?* He came back for finals! He didn't want to lose a year's credit! . . . Hey, listen, we have to talk." She took Madame Tessier's arm. Madame Tessier seemed surprised by this breech of authority, but Laura held onto her firmly and didn't let go. They went into a small side room. Laura confronted her. Her heart was thumping rapidly.

"Listen, I—uh—I know all about what happened between you and Alex . . . but that's all over now. You understand that, don't you?"

Madame Tessier smiled condescendingly. Shit, why was she so pretty? "You're being naïve, Laura. It's perfectly understandable, of course. You're a twenty-year-old American schoolgirl and I'm—"

"Okay," Laura said breathlessly, "I know! You're lonely, your husband dumped you, you have all these pressures running the school, and—"

"The fact is," Madame Tessier said, looking her right in the eye, "Alex fell in love with a French woman who understands him intellectually and who can also satisfy his romantic nature. A woman whose—"

"Who's flipped!" Laura gasped. This was worse than she had expected! She looked around nervously. "Madame Tessier, I think there's something you still don't understand—"

"Yes?"

Laura swung open the door to the storage closet and quickly shoved Madame Tessier into it. "You keep your paws off of Alex," she said. "We're going to Greece!" With a final burst of strength she pushed the door closed and latched it. Madame Tessier began pounding on the door.

Jesus! I better get out of here. Laura hurried

away. God, if only she would stay in there for the next month!

* * *

Who had parents like these? Who? Did they have to pull their Jewish-mother-and-father bit right in the middle of his first play? Couldn't they at least wait until it was over?

"Souvenirs I can understand," his mother was saying. "But taking a French *girl* home with you?"

His father tried to take a more "rational" approach. "Joel, we've never had to worry about you being sensible."

"Even when you were ten," his mother interjected, "you weren't ten, you were like a little forty-year-old man."

"That's the problem!" Joel exclaimed, exasperated. "I've never taken any risks. Isn't that why you wanted me to come to Europe? To crawl out of my shell—"

"Well, now it's time to crawl back in," his mother said. "Enough is enough. Who is this girl anyway? What is her background?"

"She's a music student," Joel said. "She's studying the flute. She plays for a chamber orchestra."

His parents were both looking at him with the same "a likely story" expression.

"Look, would you feel better if I said she's a hooker who snared me by pouring absinthe in my tea? I love her, okay? *She* loves *me*. It happens once in a while, remember? It's what makes the world go round."

"Love is something," his mother began. "Love is a *mature* emotion. Love is *not* sex!"

"Well," his father said, "sex is part of it. No, Joel, here's the point. We're delighted, naturally, that you've had this romantic encounter. It's splendid, but—"

"Splendid?" his mother said, horrified.

"Essie, hush a minute . . . We're delighted, but now you have to face real life. You're a student. You have no means of support. How will you live? What do you really know about each other? I'm sure you've had some wonderful times together, but—"

"Dad, listen to me a second, will you?" Joel said desperately. "I *love* Toni. Do you understand that? It's *not* just sex. The sex is terrific, but she's a wonderful *person!* She's kind and funny and sweet and warm and—"

His mother sighed. "Oh, Joel."

"Why 'Oh, Joel'?"

His father said, "Look, what your mother means is this. You're terribly naïve, Joel. This is your first girl friend. How can you possibly evaluate a relationship on the basis of no experience?"

"I've read a lot," he said sheepishly.

"Precisely!" his father said. "And experienced nothing. So naturally the first pretty girl that comes along and—"

"Dad, Jesus, that is *not what* happened! Don't either of you give me any credit for *anything?* I'm not a dodo! I can tell one thing from another. Toni is *not* just any girl, and this is *not* just a first romance and all that garbage. This is the real thing!"

"At twenty we all feel it's the real thing," his father said dryly.

"You've just forgotten what it's like," Joel said accusingly. "If you ever knew to begin with!"

"I have not forgotten," his father said. "Look, I was in love at twenty."

"You were?" Joel and his mother said in unison.

"Yes, with a perfectly charming, delightful girl named Cynthia Wilson."

"You never even mentioned her," Joel's mother said in wonderment.

"She was lovely!" his father said dreamily. "Five feet tall with long, crinkly blond hair and blue-green eyes. She was a little bowlegged. She'd wanted to be a dancer, but they discovered . . . Anyway, to make a long story short, it was a wonderful, wonderful experience, one I wouldn't have missed for the world, but it wasn't . . . the real thing."

"In what way wasn't it?" Joel said. "It sounds like it was."

His father looked flustered. "Well, I mean, she was just eighteen. Neither of us had ever— It could never—"

"Fred, it's amazing you never mentioned this," his mother said.

"It's not important," his father said.

"She sounds great to me," Joel said.

"Well, she was a very lovely, sensitive girl. Like

Toni, perhaps. But she had a great many problems. You see, her father deserted the family when she was nine and her mother— Well, none of that's relevant."

"What happened to her?" Joel said.

"Cynthia? She got married. I saw her ten years ago when I was back in Evanston on a business trip."

"You did?" said his mother.

"What was she like?" Joel asked, interested.

His father looked reflective. "Still lovely. Rather unhappy, though. Her husband was having affairs and she had just lost her job. She teaches art at a local community college. It was touching, in a way. She was sure if she'd married me, her life would have turned out differently."

"Maybe it would have," Joel said. He decided he liked his father more than he thought he had.

"Fred, I don't know," his mother said. "Is she the only one? Or are there dozens of other Cynthias you've never mentioned that you see on business trips?"

"There was only one Cynthia," his father said, a little regretfully.

"And did you sleep with her on this famous reunion?" his mother demanded.

"No," he said, even more regretfully. "Somehow—well . . ."

"We were talking about Joel," his mother said. "Joel, how about your career? You were going to work on *The New York Times*."

"Maybe I'll be a playwright instead."

"Well, I've got news for you. The play's the pits."

"What're you suddenly, a roving critic?"

"Look, Joel, consider the trip to Finland," his father intervened. "You don't have to decide anything final about Toni. She won't vanish into thin air. But the trip will give us a chance to sit down and discuss it all rationally and calmly."

"I'm *not* going to Finland!" Joel exploded. "I'm going back tomorrow with Toni! I've made up my mind!" He raced off down the hall with both of them at his heels. Suddenly he stopped, hearing a pounding from inside a closet. He unbolted the door; to his amazement Madame Tessier was standing inside.

She stepped forward, seeming unruffled, and extended her hand to them. "I'm Madame Tessier," she said calmly. "Director of the institute. Welcome to France."

*   *   *

The applause after the show was overwhelming. There was a standing ovation for the actors. Joel stood to one side of the stage, listening to the cheering and whistling. Finally Melanie came to get him.

"We did it!" he said, face aglow. "This is the greatest moment of my life to date!"

She pulled him onstage. He stared dumbfounded, at the cheering audience. He bowed. His parents were sitting there, beaming. Their Jewish-parent genes seemed to have moved in the ascendancy again: my son, the playwright. But as he moved offstage he saw Toni having an animated argument with *her* parents. Uh-oh!

"Monsieur Levert," Joel said, going over to them. "Madame Levert? I was just looking for your daughter."

Her father shook his hand.

"Did you—uh—enjoy the play?" Joel said, trying to smile charmingly.

Her father looked worse than *his* father. He slammed Joel against the wall. "You are *not* taking Toni to America!"

"Not you too!" Joel gasped.

"We have thought it over," Monsieur Levert said. "The more we thought, the more we worry. You have no money, she has no money, and we are not giving you any!"

A conspiracy of parents! "I love your daughter," he said, hardly having the energy to go through it again.

"Love!" Monsieur Levert gesticulated. "Love! You are twenty! What do you know of love?"

Joel sighed. "I don't know," he said. "I just don't . . . What can I say? I'll take wonderful care of her. I'll do anything, I'll—"

"My dear young man," Monsieur Levert said. "No one questions your good intentions. Your intentions are magnificent. But my daughter is French. She is a serious music student. We are concerned for her future, you understand?"

"Me too," Joel said. "I have it all planned out. You see, she can study in New York. There's this great flute teacher there, my parents know him—"

"Who? His name?"

"I can't remember, but he would love to have Toni as a student. He would get her a job with the best orchestra. It would be wonderful for her career." *God, I'm doing this so well!* he thought in amazement.

They were looking at him thoughtfully. "Well, that throws a different light on the matter," Monsieur Levert said. "Perhaps—Toni mentioned that your parents were here. Perhaps we could have a talk with them."

Joel swallowed. "Well—uh—sure. The thing is, just don't mention this teacher, because he—he had an affair with my mother once and so—" He couldn't *believe* he had just said that.

Monsieur Levert smiled. "I understand. I will be discreet. They are off there, you say?"

When they had moved off, Melanie came back and dragged him along with her.

"I don't know," Joel said. "I just plain don't know."

"*What* don't you know?"

"I don't know *anything!* There is not *one* thing in the world that I know with any certainty."

"Joel, come on, don't freak out. Just because your play's a success!"

He sighed. "It's not the play."

"What *is* it, then?"

"Everything! Life!"

She shook her head. "You're a hopeless case, you know that?"

15

It was nighttime. A tacky French combo was playing imitation American rock. The chairs had been cleared from the auditorium and the lights turned low. Tables around the edge of the auditorium were populated with institute kids, friends, and French families eating and drinking. Alex stood at the bar, waiting for his drink. Suddenly he felt a light tap on his shoulder. Turning, he saw Madame Tessier.

"Alex?"

In the soft light, in that low-cut black dress, she looked incredibly, unbelievably beautiful. "Uh—bonjour . . . bonsoir?"

"I wanted to talk to you," she said softly, tentatively.

"Well—uh—I was going to take these drinks back to—Laura's waiting and—"

"Dance with me," she said, smiling up at him.

"Dance?" He stood there, confused, frowning. She put out her hand. He hesitated a moment, then set his drink down and followed her onto the dance floor.

The music was fast; they danced apart. He stared, bewildered, as she danced. It was like the dance she had done at the jeans store, months before, charming, graceful. Only this time her eyes were fixed on him, as though to say: "This is for you." Slowly, she moved closer to him.

Mesmerized, Alex took her hand and put his arm around her. They started dancing close and more slowly, even though the music hadn't changed. My God, what's going on? he thought. What's happening? Her body seemed to melt into his as she pressed against him. Jesus! Helplessly he glanced over at Laura. She was staring at him with an absolutely stricken face. He tried to gesture an "I don't know what's happening" look, but she turned away.

It was as though there were two of him. Somewhere floating way above the clouds was a small quiet voice saying: This is *crazy!* What are you doing? Cut it out! But that part of him, the "rational" part, if that was what it was, seemed to have no power whatever over the rest of him. If someone had said, "If you don't stop dancing with her, I'm going to shoot you in cold blood," he would have kept on dancing. What had happened to his will? And why was she doing this? To torment him? Why here, in front of everyone? He had been back for weeks. Why hadn't she taken him aside and, if . . . What did she want of him? Did she really want him as her lover? I'm going to die, he thought. I'm going to die right here on the dance floor.

Everything they had done together drifted inexorably through his mind. The large bed, her kisses, her soft hands caressing his body, her eyes looking up at him. I can't stand this, he thought. What should I do? Take her somewhere and make love to her? Is that what she wants? What *does* she want?

Laura! God, how I can *do* this to her? "I'm trusting you, so be trustworthy." Getting him back into school. "Why did she give you an A?" If she weren't so beautiful, if they hadn't almost done it and had to stop, if she didn't have that hauntingly lovely expression in her eyes, if her skin wasn't white and glowing, if she wasn't wearing this incredible perfume, if she hadn't put on that dress that bared her shoulders and showed the lovely outline of her breasts, if he wasn't crazy, if for whatever insane reason being close to her like this didn't deprive him of any sense, reason, ability to act . . .

They had their arms around each other. Why didn't everything fade away except them? Why were there people here? I want us to be alone. I want them all to go away. I'll lead her somewhere and she'll take her dress off and . . .

"Alex," she said in a whisper.

"Yes?"

"I missed you so much."

"I . . . missed you." Laura, please, forgive me.

"If only I had acted differently that night. I acted so badly. I feel ashamed when I think of it."

"Well, I guess seeing your husband sort of . . . got you upset."

"I didn't want to hide anything . . . If he has his little adventures, why shouldn't I? We, at least, have so much in common, whereas he—"

So much in common! "I went away to try and forget you," he said. "I had an awful trip. I thought about you all the time."

"I thought about you . . . I was so sad that you went away without seeing me."

"I couldn't face you, it was too—"

"I was afraid you thought I didn't care for you, that I was just using you somehow."

"Well—"

"Everything is so much more complicated when you're married! Your allegiances, your ties. It's not so simple as at twenty."

"It's not so simple at twenty."

"Now you have Laura."

Laura? Who was Laura? "Yeah, only—"

"She is very much in love with you, I can see that."

"Not after this. She's—"

"You needed someone, she offered herself, I understand."

"It wasn't exactly like that," he murmured. His powers of speech and reasoning seemed distinctly impaired. Besides, the last thing in the world he wanted to think about right now was Laura. "Can we go somewhere?" he said desperately. "To be alone, I mean?"

"Yes," she murmured. "We have to be alone."

She looked up at him and, unable to resist the impulse, he bent down and kissed her on the lips. The small voice in his head said: You're being watched by two hundred people. You're out of your mind!

She walked off the dance floor and he followed her numbly, in a trance, not looking at anything around him, not wanting to see if Laura was still there. They ended up in the darkened music room. He put his arms around her and kissed her passionately. "Can we—"

"Alex, we have to talk," she said in a strangled voice.

"We do?"

"Yes."

"I don't know if I—I'm not thinking too clearly right now." He tried to smile.

She was staring at him gravely. "We were very indiscreet just now."

Alex swallowed. "Yeah, I—"

"I'm afraid I exercised very bad judgment, behaving that way in front of the other students. I feel ashamed." She gazed down at the floor.

"They'll forget all about it tomorrow," he said. Laura won't.

"It's not just the reputation of the school that worries me," she said, "but your friend—"

"She'll understand," he said lightly.

"Will she? That's very understanding . . . I've thought of a way you can stay here with me. Would you like that?"

"Sure, but how?"

She crossed the dark room and turned on a lamp

by a piano. She sat on the piano bench and took a letter out of her purse. Unfolding it, she started reading: " 'Dear Mr. and Mrs. Jensen: As per our telephone conversation, I am—' "

"Telephone? You called my *parents?*"

"Not yet. I'm going to. Shh. 'I am writing concerning your son, Alex, who I want to employ at my Institute for French Studies.' "

"You do?"

"Yes, that's my plan. Sit down."

He sat down tentatively on the edge of a couch.

" 'There is a summer session starting immediately, and Alex would be acting as a counselor for the American students and as my personal assistant. Now, why Alex, you ask? Well, Alex is intelligent and, when motivated, an excellent scholar.' " She smiled at him ironically. "So, that's a little lie. 'He is also very attractive physically and can be quite charming, especially to women. His sense of humor can change suddenly into something very tender and soft, like the touch of his fingers. I remember the first night Alex and I were alone together—' "

Alex felt panicked. "Listen, let me read the rest to myself." He frowned when he was done. "Uh— Madame Tessier? I don't think you should send this letter to my parents."

"Why not?"

"Because it's a little too . . . revealing." He hesitated. "And, actually, I'm not sure this whole thing is really a first-rate idea."

She looked surprised. "I think it is. I've thought

about it a lot. Why not?" She reached for the letter and took it back.

Alex spoke slowly. "I appreciate the offer—the job," he said, "but I—don't think I can stay."

Madame Tessier frowned. "You are hurt, is that it? You don't think I really care for you?"

"It's not that, it's just—"

"What about everything? What about the song you wrote me?"

"That was just a song. I didn't think—I mean, this is really happening here." He felt stupid and inarticulate.

"You told me you wanted to experience life."

He smiled. "I've had enough experience. Plenty. Right now I'm just going to travel a little this summer and then go back to Ohio. It's very quiet there. I think I need to recuperate from—all my experiences."

A sad expression crossed her face. Then she shrugged casually. "Okay. Well, I can always . . . find another assistant. So what? I can use this same letter. I'll just change the name and—"

He was touched at the hurt quality in her voice. He went over and put his arms around her and held her tenderly.

"I don't really need an assistant," she said in a soft, breathless voice. "I can't afford it anyway."

"I'm sorry," Alex said, touching her smooth, shiny hair.

She looked up at him. "When you go back, will you tell your friends about the institute?"

"Oh, I will," Alex said. "Don't worry."

"Will you tell about me?"

"No," he said. "I won't tell anyone about you."

She stood there quietly for a few moments, letting herself be held. Then she moved away. "Next fall our students will have a choice of the Paris campus or the new one in Florence." Her voice sounded brisk and professional again.

"Sounds great," Alex said, trying to fall in with her tone.

They moved out of the music room and down the hall. "You know, the tuition is cheaper in Italy," she went on. "Plus we will provide a winter side trip to the Alps. Skis and boots are not included."

He stopped at the stairs and looked at her. There was an awkward pause. She put out her hand. Alex took it. "I guess I better go now," he said with some difficulty.

As he went down the steps, she continued talking. "Alex, keep in touch. We have a newsletter and we write about anything interesting that happens to our students after they leave."

Alex stopped on the staircase and looked back at her. "Madame Tessier," he said, "it'll be a long time before anything this interesting happens to me. But I'll let you know ... *Au revoir*."

She smiled at him. "*Ciao*, Alex."

He felt her eyes on him as he walked the rest of the way down.

* * *

Joel was standing outside the dance hall, when Laura came out.

"Oh, hi, Joel," she said breathlessly. "Listen, what time are you and Toni leaving tomorrow?"

"I don't know," Joel said. "I can't find her."

"I'll call you. We'll go to the airport together."

"What about Greece? Alex told me you were—" He stopped at her stricken face. "I'm sorry," he said gently. "Well, you know how Alex gets."

She raised her chin high. "Not with me!"

"I'll help you find a cab."

After he put her in a cab he went to search for Toni. He found her in a dark corner sipping a drink.

"Where are your parents?" he said.

"Talking to yours."

"Jesus."

"What is this with Alex and Madame Tessier?"

"I don't know! He went bananas."

"Poor Laura."

"Yeah."

"Where did they go?"

He shrugged. "I hate to imagine . . . Listen, Toni, let's just get out of here, okay?"

"But our parents—"

"I'm sick of our parents! Come on! Let's get out through the garden." He took her hand and they rushed into the dark, cool night. Just as they got there, the voice of his father came drifting out. "Joel, are you out there?"

"Oh shit!" Joel said. He pulled Toni past the

classical statues in the garden that stood like grave white presences in the night, down to the gate; it was locked. He rattled it. "Oh no! Okay, let's go over the wall, then!"

"Toni, *où es tu?*" came Toni's father's voice. *"Nous devons discuter—"*

"Climb up the trellis," Joel said. "Quick!"

She stepped up onto the trellis and swung her leg over the top of the fence. Joel followed her and they both straddled the fence.

"There they are!" his mother shrieked. "They're over there playing on the fence."

"We're not playing, Mother," Joel said.

The four parents moved in on them.

"Well, what are you doing?" his mother demanded.

"Get down, Joel," his father said. "We just came to talk."

"What shall we do?" Toni whispered in a frightened voice. "I'm scared."

"Give me your hand. I'll lower you."

"I'm scared!"

"Who isn't?"

Toni's father was talking in rapid, furious French.

"Joel, what's he saying?" his mother said.

"I don't know."

"Didn't you learn *anything* this year? Whatever he's saying, he's right!"

"Are you sure?" Toni asked anxiously.

"Sure!" Joel said. "Let go of my leg, Dad!" He

tried to kick off his father's hold and was thrown off balance. With a sudden slide he toppled off the fence and hurtled to the ground.

"Joel, are you all right?" Toni said, bending over him.

Joel tried to get up. It hurt, but he moved tentatively toward her. "Toni, don't fail me now."

"But are you positive?"

"Yes, I'm positive, damn it. I love you!"

Toni smiled. She swung her leg over the fence and Joel helped her down. She kissed him gently on the lips. "Me too," she said.

Through the gate, Joel could hear his father calling, "Joel, remember, we warned you. You're making a big mistake."

Toni hurried over and kissed her mother through the gate.

"I'm doing the first spontaneous, irrational, unpredictable thing I've ever done in my life," Joel said wildly. He pulled Toni back and they waved.

"But what if it's a bad idea?" his mother called.

Joel just shrugged and smiled. Holding Toni's hand, he went off with her down the alley.

*   *   *

Laura walked swiftly through the airport terminal with Joel and Toni at her side. Suddenly, to her horror, she looked up and saw Alex coming toward them. She rushed ahead to avoid him, but heard him talking to Joel.

"What're you doing here?" Joel was asking. "Are you going back?"

"No, I'm staying," Alex said. "I came to say goodbye."

Firmly Laura put her bag on the conveyor belt. She glanced at Alex coldly as they passed through the metal detectors. As the bags came off the conveyor, Alex suddenly grabbed her bag. Laura looked at him indignantly. "That's mine!"

"I know."

"Let me have it, please."

"Not till you let me explain."

"There's nothing to explain."

"There is." He grabbed her arm and stared at her intensely. "Laura, please, just give me five minutes, okay?"

"No!"

Alex trotted after her toward the ticket area, holding her bag.

"Did you get your boarding passes?" he asked Joel.

"No," Joel said, "I'll get them."

Laura turned to Alex and grabbed angrily at her bag. "I need my ticket!"

He reached into her bag and handed her the ticket envelope. She snatched it out of his hand and walked with Joel to the counter. Alex put her bag down and just stood there, staring at her, an uncertain expression on his face. Fuck him! Now suddenly he wanted to kiss and make up after that scene last night. No sir. At the ticket counter,

Laura handed the ticket agent her envelope. "Same flight," she said. "New York."

The man pulled the ticket out of the envelope and inspected it curiously. Annoyed, he smiled coldly at her. "I'm sorry," he said. "This is not for Flight 35."

Laura frowned. "What do you mean?"

"Mademoiselle" he said impatiently. "This is not even a plane ticket. You have two *train* tickets here."

Laura stared down at the tickets, dumbfounded. "Two *train*—"

"And they are not for New York. They are for Geneva, Venice, Belgrade, Athens."

Laura looked over at Alex. She marched up to him.

"I just thought you'd rather go to Greece," he said, smiling sheepishly.

"You did, huh?"

"Don't you?"

"With you?"

He nodded. There was a pleading look in his eyes. She felt her heart flip over. She stared at him intently. "What, exactly, happened last night? I'll give you five minutes for a true explanation. True!"

He swallowed. "Okay. This is what happened. When we danced together, I went crazy. I felt madly attracted to her again; I couldn't help myself. I wanted to make love to her on the spot. I followed her into the music room. Right away she was cool again. 'Not now, later.' I thought: The *hell*

217

with this! It's the same fucking story all over again! She said, 'I want you to stay in Paris for another year. I'll write your parents.' I said, nicely of course, 'Thanks, but no thanks.' She looked hurt. I didn't regret it." He sighed. "*That's* what happened, Laura."

She knew he had told the truth. "Okay."

"Okay, what?"

"Are you asking me to forgive you?"

"Yes."

"I do." She smiled painfully. "That thing last night was the worst thing that *ever* happened to me. Absolutely the worst. I can't tell you—"

He reached out and took her hand. "I'm so sorry."

"I felt like I was going to die," she said, gazing at him.

"Laura." His voice was shaking. "I love you."

"No, you don't."

"I do . . . I really do. I wanted her physically, but that's different. I mean, I want you that way too, but there's more. It's different."

She tried to smile. "*You* are a complicated person. Did anyone ever tell you that?"

He smiled back. "You're not?"

"I guess we both are."

He leaned over, took her in his arms, and kissed her. It was a long, passionate kiss. Joel came over to them.

"Hey, break it up! Or I'll call the cops."

They turned and smiled at him. "I guess I'm going to Greece," Laura said.

"Let's keep in touch," Alex said.

"Definitely," Joel said. "Take care, both of you."

"You too," they said in unison.

"You know what we should do now?" Alex said when Joel had moved off.

"I can think of a couple of things," Laura said.

He smiled. "We should have a wonderful expensive lunch at a three-star restaurant."

"Alex! You're crazy."

"Of course. Did I ever say I wasn't? . . . In fact, I've made reservations for one o'clock."

She burst out laughing. "Sure of yourself, aren't you? What if I'd gotten on the plane?"

"I knew you wouldn't." As they walked off, arm in arm, he went on. "And then we'll go back to my place and make passionate love all afternoon."

"Well, it sounds like the best offer I've gotten this morning," Laura said. "I accept."

"It's your blond hair," he said. "I can't resist round-hipped blonds with green eyes."

"I don't have green eyes! And my hips—well, okay."

She felt very happy.

*   *   *

Joel and Toni walked down the moving runway of the airport. Toni was slightly ahead of him. Joel turned. He saw a line of kids gliding toward him from the other direction. They seemed excited and bewildered. He looked around. At the end of the moving runway Christine came running up to meet

219

the new arrivals. Madame Tessier followed, trying to look in command. She was holding a sign which read: *Institute for French Studies*. It was upside down.

Joel smiled. Then he turned. Toni was far ahead of him. She looked back and beckoned for him. For one second he had a moment of panic. Then he started forward to join her.

ABOUT THE AUTHOR

NORMA KLEIN grew up in New York City and received a B.A. from Barnard College and an M.A. in Slavic languages from Columbia in 1963. At that time she decided to devote herself full time to writing and has done so since.

Ms. Klein's many adult novels include *It's OK If You Don't Love Me* and *Love Is One of the Choices*. She is also the author of several books for young people. She lives in New York City with her husband and two daughters.

FREE
Fawcett Books Listing

There is Romance, Mystery, Suspense, and Adventure waiting for you inside the Fawcett Books Order Form. And it's yours to browse through and use to get all the books you've been wanting . . . but possibly couldn't find in your bookstore.

This easy-to-use order form is divided into categories and contains over 1500 titles by your favorite authors.

So don't delay—take advantage of this special opportunity to increase your reading pleasure.

Just send us your name and address and 35¢ (to help defray postage and handling costs).

If you liked the movie, you'll love the book!

FRENCH POSTCARDS   14297-3 $2.25
by Norma Klein

An utterly charming story of mischief and romance in Paris, written with the same warm sensitivity that Norma Klein has brought to her other bestselling Fawcett novels IT'S OK IF YOU DON'T LOVE ME and LOVE IS ONE OF THE CHOICES.

THE IN-LAWS   14252-3 $1.95
by David Rogers

The hilarious tale of a prime crime and young love in search of a motel. From the Warner Brothers motion picture starring Peter Falk and Alan Arkin.

CAPRICORN ONE   14024-5 $1.75
by Ron Goulart

To all appearances the launching of Capricorn One, the first spaceship to Mars, seemed perfectly normal. But behind the scenes, a NASA director was warning the three astronauts that their spacecraft was faulty. For them, a special fate had been arranged. . . .

ICE CASTLES   14154-3 $1.95
by Leonore Fleischer

Alexis Winston was a beautiful young woman with a dream— to become a champion figure skater. She was also in love with Nick, her childhood sweetheart, who had some dreams of his own. . . . Some dreams are shattered. Some come true.